A Vote for Murder

A *Murder, She Wrote* MYSTERY

A Vote for Murder

A *Murder, She Wrote* MYSTERY

A NOVEL BY
JESSICA FLETCHER & DONALD BAIN

Based on the Universal television series created by
Peter S. Fischer, Richard Levinson & William Link

NEW AMERICAN LIBRARY

New American Library
Published by New American Library, a division of
Penguin Group (USA) Inc., 375 Hudson Street,
New York, New York 10014, USA
Penguin Group (Canada), 10 Alcorn Avenue, Toronto,
Ontario M4V 3B2, Canada (a division of Pearson Penguin Canada Inc.)
Penguin Books Ltd., 80 Strand, London WC2R 0RL, England
Penguin Ireland, 25 St. Stephen's Green, Dublin 2,
Ireland (a division of Penguin Books Ltd.)
Penguin Group (Australia), 250 Camberwell Road, Camberwell, Victoria 3124,
Australia (a division of Pearson Australia Group Pty. Ltd.)
Penguin Books India Pvt. Ltd., 11 Community Centre, Panchsheel Park,
New Delhi - 110 017, India
Penguin Group (NZ), Cnr Airborne and Rosedale Roads, Albany,
Auckland 1310, New Zealand (a division of Pearson New Zealand Ltd.)
Penguin Books (South Africa) (Pty.) Ltd., 24 Sturdee Avenue,
Rosebank, Johannesburg 2196, South Africa

Penguin Books Ltd, Registered Offices:
80 Strand, London WC2R 0RL, England

First published by New American Library,
a division of Penguin Group (USA) Inc.

First Printing, October 2004
10 9 8 7 6 5 4 3 2 1

 REGISTERED TRADEMARK—MARCA REGISTRADA

LIBRARY OF CONGRESS CATALOGING-IN-PUBLICATION DATA:

Bain, Donald, 1935–
A vote for murder : a Murder, she wrote mystery : a novel / by Jessica Fletcher & Donald Bain.
p. cm.
"Based on the Universal television series created by Peter S. Fischer,
Richard Levinson & William Link."
ISBN 0-451-21303-3
1. Fletcher, Jessica (Fictitious character)—Fiction. 2. Women politicians—Crimes against—
Fiction. 3. Literacy programs—Fiction. 4. Washington (D.C.)—Fiction.
5. Women novelists—Fiction.

I. Murder, she wrote (Television program) II. Title.
PS3552.A376V68 2004
813'.54—dc22   2004009316

Set in Minion
Designed by Ginger Legato

Printed in the United States of America

PUBLISHER'S NOTE
This is a work of fiction. Names, characters, places, and incidents either are the product of the author's imagination or are used fictitiously, and any resemblance to actual persons, living or dead, business establishments, events, or locales is entirely coincidental.

For Sylvan James Paley—welcome to the world.

A Vote
for
Murder

A *Murder, She Wrote* Mystery

Chapter One

The White House?"

"Yes. A reception there."

I was enjoying breakfast at Mara's Waterfront Luncheonette with my friends Dr. Seth Hazlitt, and Cabot Cove's sheriff, Mort Metzger. It was a gloomy early August day, thick gray clouds hovering low over the dock, the humidity having risen overnight to an uncomfortable level.

"When are you leaving?" Seth asked after taking the last bite of his blueberry pancakes, Mara's signature breakfast dish at her popular eatery.

"Day after tomorrow," I said.

"I don't envy you, Mrs. F," said Mort.

"Why?"

"August in Washington, D.C.? Maureen and I were there about this time last year. Never been so hot in my life."

I laughed and sipped my tea. "I'm sure the air-conditioning will be working just fine," I said.

"Ayuh," Seth said. "I don't expect they let the president sweat a whole lot. Or U.S. senators, for that matter."

Warren Nebel, Maine's junior senator, had arranged for my trip to Washington. He'd invited me to join three other writers in our nation's capital to help celebrate a national literacy program at the Library of Congress. I'd eagerly accepted, of course. And when Senator Nebel included a reception at the White House on our first evening there, my heart raced a little with anticipation.

I don't believe that anyone, no matter how sophisticated, worldly, well connected, or wealthy, doesn't feel at least a twinge of excitement when invited to the White House to meet the president of the United States. I am certainly no exception. It wouldn't be my first time at the People's House, although it had been a few years since my last visit. Adding to the excitement were the writers with whom I'd be spending the week, distinguished authors all, some of whom I'd been reading and enjoying for years, and I looked forward to actually shaking hands and chatting with them. Writers, with some notable exceptions, tend to be solitary creatures, not especially comfortable in social situations. I suppose it has a lot to do with the private nature of how we work, sitting alone for months at a time, sometimes years, working on a book, with only spasmodic human interaction. Those who break out and become public personalities often end up so enamored of the experience that writing goes by the boards. I've always tried to balance my life between the necessary hibernation to get a book done, and joining the rest of the world when between writing projects. That was my situation when I received the invitation from Senator Nebel—a book recently completed and off to the publisher, and free time on my hands. Perfect timing.

Our little breakfast confab ended suddenly when both Seth and Mort received calls on their cell phones, prompting them to leave in a hurry, Seth to the hospital for an emergency admission, Mort to the scene of an auto accident on the highway outside of town. Seth tried to grab the bill from the table, but I was quicker: "Please," I said. "It's my treat. Go on now. Emergencies can't wait."

I wasn't alone at the table very long because Mara, the luncheonette's gregarious proprietor, joined me.

"Hear you're going to Washington to give the president some good advice," she said, blowing away a wisp of hair from her forehead. She'd come from the kitchen; a sheen of perspiration covered her face.

"I'm sure he doesn't need any advice from me," I said.

"Not so sure about that," she said. "Going alone?"

"To Washington? Yes."

"Thought you might be taking Doc Hazlitt with you."

"I'd love to have him accompany me, but—"

"Shame you won't have a companion to share it with you, Jess."

"Oh, I really won't be alone. I . . ."

Mara's cocked head, and her narrowed eyes said she expected more from me. Besides being a wonderful cook and hostess at her establishment, she's Cabot Cove's primary conduit of gossipy information. She not only knows everyone in town; she seems to be privy to their most private thoughts and activities.

"I'll be meeting George," I said casually, making a point of picking up the bill and scrutinizing it.

"George?"

"Yes," I said, pulling cash from my purse. "George Sutherland."

"That Scotland Yard fella you met in London years ago?"

"That's right," I replied, standing and brushing crumbs from my skirt. "He'll be there attending an international conference on terrorism. Just a coincidence. Breakfast was great, Mara. Bye-bye."

The last words I heard from Mara as I pushed open the door—and she headed back to the kitchen—were, "You are a sly one, Jessica Fletcher."

I chided myself on my walk home for having mentioned George Sutherland. Knowing Mara, half the town would have heard about it by noon, the other half by dinnertime. Mara didn't mean any harm with her penchant for gossip, nor was she the only one. Charlene Sassi's bakery is another source of juicy scuttlebutt. (What is it about places with food that seem to spawn hearsay?) Small towns like my beloved Cabot Cove thrive on rumors, and in almost every case they're utterly harmless. As far as George Sutherland was concerned, there had been plenty of speculation that he and I had become romantically involved since meeting during a murder investigation in England. There was no basis to those rumors, although he'd expressed interest in advancing our relationship to another level, and I'd not found the contemplation unpleasant. But after some serious talks during those times when we managed to be together, we decided that neither this handsome Scottish widower, nor this Cabot Cove widow were ready for a more intimate involvement, and contented ourselves with frequent letters, occasional long-distance phone calls, and chance meetings when our schedules brought us together.

The rain started just as I reached my house. I picked up the local newspaper that had been delivered while I was gone, ducked inside, closed some windows, made myself a cup of tea, and reviewed the package of information Senator Nebel's office had sent, accompanied by a letter from the senator.

It promised to be a whirlwind week in Washington, and I added to my packing list an extra pair of comfortable walking shoes. The reception at the White House was scheduled for five o'clock the day I arrived. Following it, Senator Nebel would host a dinner at his home. The ensuing days were chockablock with meetings and seminars at the Library of Congress, luncheons and dinners with notables from government and the publishing industry, and other assorted official and social affairs. Why event planners think they must fill every waking moment has always escaped me; everyone appreciates a little downtime in the midst of a hectic week. My concern, however, was that I wouldn't find time to enjoy again being in George Sutherland's company. It had been a long while since we'd last seen each other, our schedules making it difficult for him to come to the States from London, where he was a senior Scotland Yard inspector, or for me to cross the Atlantic in the opposite direction. It had been *too* long, and

I didn't want to squander the opportunity of being in the same city at the same time.

When I picked up the newspaper, a headline on the front page caught my eye: NEBEL'S VOTE ON POWER PLANT STILL UNCERTAIN.

The battle within the Senate over the establishment of a new, massive nuclear power plant in Maine, only twenty miles outside Cabot Cove, had been in the news for weeks. From what I'd read, the Senate was almost equally split between those in favor of the plant, and those opposed. Its proponents claimed it was vitally necessary to avoid the sort of widespread blackouts the East Coast had experienced since the late fifties, five of them since 1959, including the biggest of them all in 2003. Senator Nebel, who'd pledged to fight the plant during his most recent campaign, had pointed to the enormous cost, not to mention the ecological threat the plant posed to our scenic state, and further condemned the lobbyists behind the project and their clients, large multistate electric power companies that would benefit handsomely from the plant's construction. Some members of President David Dimond's cabinet had enjoyed strong ties to those companies prior to entering public service.

But the article claimed that Nebel's opposition to the plant could no longer be taken for granted, according to unnamed Washington insiders. The piece ended with: *Reports that Senator Nebel has recently received death threats are unconfirmed, although unnamed sources close to the senator say that security has been beefed up for him, both on Capitol Hill and at his home.*

Death threats! Usually they came from demented people who have no intention of carrying through on them. But you can never take that for granted, and every such threat must be taken seriously. I knew one thing: Our junior senator had chosen a contentious time to be hosting a literacy program at the Library of Congress. Was there ever a time when something important, something potentially earth-shattering, wasn't going on somewhere in the world, and by extension in Washington, D.C.? I doubted it.

I replaced that weighty thought with a more pleasant one: visiting the White House and meeting the president, spending time with some of my fellow writers, and, of course, touching base in person with George Sutherland.

Chapter Two

Ah, Jessica Fletcher, Maine's very own Agatha Christie."

Senator Warren Nebel crossed the room, hands extended, a dazzling smile painted across his square, tanned face. "But Dame Agatha could never hold a candle to you," he added, to my discomfort.

"How nice to see you again, Senator," I said, losing my hand in both of his. "Thank you so much for including me in this exciting week."

"What would a literacy program be without someone of your stature?" he said in a voice loud enough for others in the vicinity to hear.

We were in the White House's Blue Room, an oval room the same size as the president's Oval Office, and one of the residence's main formal reception rooms. The chairs and a sofa, a mixture of originals and reproductions of a Parisian gilt suite ordered for the room in 1817 by

President Monroe, were covered in a lovely blue fabric. Blue drapes framed soaring windows; the windows themselves framed an imposing view of the Washington Monument, gleaming in the late-afternoon sun. Two lovely Fitz Hugh Lane oils of Boston and Baltimore harbors added a colorful peek at history to complement the room's appeal.

Our junior senator from Maine wasn't that junior; his campaign biography stated he was sixty-one. That our second senator, Marjorie Hale, a dynamic woman in her early seventies, had been in the Senate longer than Nebel accounted for his "junior" status. He was a handsome man, tall and lean, in good physical shape, and with a seemingly bottomless reserve of energy. The gray suit he wore was immaculately tailored, a far cry from the jeans and flannel shirts he wore when campaigning back in Maine.

I recalled that Nebel's political life had not been without scandal, although his had occurred—fortunately, it seemed—early in his career. When he was speaker of the Maine senate, he'd been caught in a compromising position with an aide with whom he'd been having a yearlong affair. His wife, Patricia, was not the sort of woman who looked the other way when confronted by such indiscretions. She filed for divorce. A few months later, to the surprise of many Maine citizens who shared her views, the couple announced they'd reconciled, and he moved back into their modest home in a neighborhood of tract homes north of town. That nasty episode behind him and forgotten—or forgiven by most voters—he ran for a vacated U.S. Senate seat and won by the narrowest of margins. He was now at the end of his second six-year term, and running hard for a third.

I'd gotten to know Patricia Nebel fairly well in Cabot Cove. We'd served together on various civic committees, including fund-raising for the Cabot Cove Free Library, a cause close to Pat's heart. I'd been a guest in her home on more than one occasion, and I'd hosted a few dinner parties at which she was present. As I got to know her better, I came to realize that she was uncomfortable in the role of politician's wife. Not that she wasn't supportive of her husband's political ambitions. To the contrary, she appeared at many of his rallies, and actively raised money for his campaigns. She was, as the saying goes, a good soldier.

But there was little doubt that given a choice, she preferred the serenity of her vegetable and flower gardens, and experimenting with recipes in her kitchen to the hurly-burly, frenetic pace of the political life. In the early days of her husband's first term as a United States senator, she accompanied him to Washington with some regularity. Those trips became less frequent as the years passed. Once, when I visited her at her home and we sat sipping iced tea in her garden, she said, "If I had my way, Jess, I'd never spend another minute of my life in Washington. Oh, I know, it's a truly beautiful city, and what happens there on a day-to-day basis impacts everyone's life, here and abroad. But I find it—shall I say it?—I find it a cruel place, at least its political side. And let's face it," she added with a laugh, "politics is Washington's major industry."

Rumors from Washington surfaced now and then in Cabot Cove that our junior senator might not have learned his earlier lesson, and was enjoying extracurricular relationships outside his marriage in the nation's capital, Washington. But those bits of gossip were generally dismissed as having been generated by political opponents, enhanced by Washington's well-known penchant for character assassination. What part they played in keeping Pat Nebel close to home remained conjecture.

Senator Nebel interrupted my reverie. "Have you been treated well since arriving?" he asked.

"Extremely," I answered with conviction.

My day had started early in Cabot Cove. Jed Richardson, a former top commercial airline pilot who'd retired to Cabot Cove to start up his own charter airline service, had flown me in a small twin-engine plane to Boston, where I connected with a jet to Washington. Jed had given me flying lessons a few years earlier, and I'd earned my private pilot's license, which most people found amusing, since I don't drive a car. I can fly a plane, but you never see me on the road behind the wheel of an automobile, as I prefer my trusty bicycle for getting around town.

Both flights had been smooth, and I arrived at Washington's Reagan National Airport at two in the afternoon, right on time. A limousine was waiting to take me to the magnificent Willard InterContinental Hotel, on Pennsylvania Avenue, where I was checked into a lovely suite. A stone's throw from the White House, the Willard had been renovated in the eighties to its original splendor as one of Washington's most imposing hospitality landmarks; over the years it had been a treasured home away from home for many heads of state and other dignitaries.

Now, a few hours after a quick nap, showering, and changing into what I thought was an appropriate outfit for a meeting with the president of the United States—a lavender silk suit and white blouse—I waited to be ushered into his office.

The person in charge of our group was Nebel's chief of staff, Nikki Farlow, a tall, attractive woman I judged to be late thirties to early forties, although I admit I'm not very good at such judgments. She wore her auburn hair short, off her neck, and had a deft hand with her makeup, tastefully applied to enhance a thin face, aquiline nose, and prominent cheekbones. She wore a severely tailored gray pantsuit and black blouse, an indication that she was all business. Her manner was pleasant enough, although it was evident that behind it was a strong, no-nonsense lady very much in command of her life and probably those of others with whom she was involved. Being a U.S. senator's top aide would demand the sense of self-assuredness she exuded, and I had no doubt that she was very good at her job. She'd been my contact as the trip drew close, and her attention to every detail, no matter how small, was impressive.

I'd been the first of our contingent to arrive. My conversation with Nebel ended when he saw others being led into the Blue Room by Secret Service agents assigned to that duty, and left me to greet a short, stocky man with a long white beard and flowing hair to match, and a middle-aged woman wearing what appeared to be a housedress that came down to her calves. Her mousy brown hair was pulled back into a severe bun; she wore black running shoes. I recognized her. Marsha Jane Grane, a revered and prolific author whose books were noted for their often violent and salacious content. Her subject matter was cause for criticism in some circles, but her reputation as a woman of letters was firmly established, with numerous literary awards to support it.

Nebel brought them to where I stood and we were introduced. The man was Karl von Miller, whose novels for young adults were among the most popular of that genre. We had only a minute to chat before the rest of our party arrived and we were ushered into the Oval Office where an exuberant President Dimond came from behind his desk and eagerly shook our hands. He was a shorter man than he appeared to be on television; I suppose the nature of television transmissions, coupled with the office he held, tended to create a sense of height and stature.

He'd obviously been well prepared. He had an appropriate thing to say to each of us about our books, the names of our most recent works coming easily off his lips, his smile never fading. He said to me, "It amazes me, Mrs. Fletcher, how you come up with intricate plots and wrap everything up so neatly at the end. Maybe I should hire you to lend that talent to this office."

I laughed along with him, then said, "I'm sure it's a lot easier to do in a book, Mr. President."

"Unfortunately, you're right," he said. "I especially enjoyed your latest work, *A Cautious Murder,* where the murderer was tripped up by his obsession with making everything orderly in his life, even the murder he committed. Neatness did him in."

"Thank you, Mr. President," I said, impressed that he'd read the book. Or had he? Had an aide fed him that line in preparation for meeting me? *Don't be so cynical*, I silently reminded myself.

By the time I'd processed that thought, he was on to the next author in line, Ms. Grane, extolling her writings as providing a clear view into the human psyche. We all received that sort of personal recognition in the fifteen minutes we were there. The meeting ended with a White House photographer snapping a photo of each of us with the president, and before we knew it, we were in limousines heading for dinner at Senator Nebel's home in McLean, Virginia.

My companions in the rear seat were Marsha Jane Grane, another writer, Bill Littlefield, author of best-selling histories of the Korean and Vietnam wars, and Nikki Farlow.

When I'd learned that George Sutherland and I would be in Washington at the same time, I summoned my courage and called Ms. Farlow to ask whether he could join us at the White House. I wasn't surprised at her answer, although her tone took me aback. She dismissed the request as impossible, lecturing me about how difficult such arrangements were, and further explaining that with security concerns paramount in this age of terrorism, adding an "outsider" was out of the question. That George was a senior Scotland Yard inspector, intimately involved in combating terrorism in Great Britain, didn't carry any weight. As I said, I didn't expect my request to be honored, but had made it under the "nothing ventured, nothing gained" philosophy. I thanked Ms. Farlow for even considering it, and dropped the matter.

Therefore, I was pleasantly surprised the next day when she called me at home to say that although Inspector Sutherland would not be able to join me at the White House, Senator Nebel had invited him to the dinner party at his home that same night. I thanked her for the courtesy and contented myself with knowing that George would, at least, be able to enjoy that aspect of the evening.

"How long have you worked with the senator?" I asked Nikki—we were now on a first-name basis—during the drive, which took us across the Potomac River and in a northerly direction, parallel to the river; the Potomac is as much a Washington landmark as many of its most famous monuments.

"I joined him two years ago," she said.

"You've always worked in government?" Littlefield asked.

"No," she said. "I ran my own head-hunting business until the senator offered me the job. I met him on a fundraising trip he'd taken through the Midwest."

"You're from there?" I asked.

"Chicago," she replied, simultaneously flipping through pages of handwritten notes on a yellow legal pad she'd removed from a briefcase. Not wanting to intrude on her official thoughts, I directed conversation to Littlefield, who'd had little to say up to that point. I'd asked him about his latest book, and he was telling me when the driver turned onto a narrow, tree-lined road that took us in the direction of the river. A minute later we followed the other limos onto a circular gravel driveway that swept in front of an imposing home on the banks of the Potomac. I was surprised at how large the house was, probably because my perception of where and how Nebel lived was shaped by my Cabot Cove experience. His home there was as modest as his campaign clothing promised.

But this was a mansion in every sense of the word. It appeared to be a structure that had been expanded numerous times, with wings jutting out in every direction without any apparent attempt to match architectural styles each time a new addition was constructed. The second floor, too, seemed to have been added at a different time, its Palladian windows in contrast to less expansive ones on the first level.

As I stepped from the limousine, I looked to my left to see a two-story garage with six bays. A silver Jaguar and a black Mercedes sat in front of it; two motorcycles were parked off to the side.

"Are those apartments over the garage?" I asked Ms. Farlow.

"Live-in household staff," she replied.

A uniformed security guard holding a clipboard stood at the massive wooden doors leading from the driveway into the house, and we were asked to identify ourselves before being allowed to enter and checked off his list. Once inside, we were in a spacious foyer with a stone floor in which slabs of granite of various hues had been embedded. Large vases of freshly cut, colorful flowers sat on heavy furniture that hugged the walls. An elaborate brass chandelier, easily seven feet in diameter, cast soft light from above. Ms. Farlow asked us to follow her from the foyer down a long hallway to a huge room at the opposite side of the house. In contrast to what I'd seen so far, the room's modernity was striking. Floor-to-ceiling windows provided a splendid view of the river, which was at least seventy-five feet down a steep slope from a wide brick terrace on the other side of the glass. A large plasma TV screen was on a wall near a conversation pit in a corner of the room. A massive stone fireplace dominated one wall; the brass handles on a set of antique fireplace tools glistened in light from recessed fixtures that dotted the high ceiling.

I went to the windows and gazed at the Potomac. A long, narrow, winding set of wooden stairs snaked from the terrace to a dock at the base where a nicely rigged, center-console fishing boat bobbed in the gentle wake of other passing craft.

"This is absolutely beautiful," I said to no one in particular.

A white-jacketed man of East Indian extraction, holding a tray on which filled champagne flutes rested, responded: "Madam?" he said.

"Yes, thank you," I said, taking one of the glasses. His eyes locked with mine, large, very dark, expressive eyes. He walked to where others had gathered, offering champagne to them, too. From another corner of the room came a woman wearing a similar outfit. She passed a tray of hors d'oeuvres—crostini with herb-whipped goat cheese and pine nuts, wasabi-rubbed New Zealand lamb chops, crab-meat herb and phyllo cigars, and wild mushroom bruschetta with shaved Parmesan. By this time, the number of people in the room had swelled, and I assumed they were either friends of Nebel's, or professional colleagues. I recognized from watching the House of Representatives on C-SPAN two members of that body, a congressman from Ohio whose fiery speeches on the floor of the House were well-known (and dismaying to some, I was sure), and a congresswoman whose base, I seemed to remember, was California, and who'd made headlines when she'd cast the deciding vote in favor of President Dimond's most recent budget proposal.

"Lovely home, isn't it?" Marsha Jane Grane said, coming up to my side at the window.

"Yes, it is. The views are spectacular."

"Do you have views where you write?" she asked.

"My backyard," I replied lightly. "Plenty of birds at my feeder."

"I work in total solitude," she said. "A view like this would keep me from concentrating. I have no windows in my writing room, only a desk, chair, and typewriter."

That led to a discussion of working on a typewriter versus a computer, or writing in longhand. I divided my attention between Ms. Grane and the door to the room, looking for George Sutherland's arrival. I was defending my choice of a computer, reluctantly at first, I admitted, and its word-processing capability, when George entered, escorted by the security guard who'd cleared us at the front door. Nikki Farlow had told me that a limousine would pick him up at his hotel and deliver him here, which it obviously had.

"Excuse me," I told Marsha Jane. "A friend of mine has just arrived."

"Jessica," George said. "You look absolutely marvelous."

"And so do you."

By any objective standards, George Sutherland was a handsome man, with a distinguished air about him. In his sixties, he stood six feet, four inches tall and carried himself with easy confidence. His hair was brown with red tinges in it; a slightly larger patch of gray at each temple than when I'd last seen him added a promise of wisdom and distinction. Fine features were nicely arranged on his large, deeply lined face. His eyes, serious but with a constant promise of mirth and bemusement at what went on around him, were the green of Granny Smith apples. I'd come to learn that his favorite clothing consisted of tweed jackets with leather at the elbows, muted ties, sleeveless pullover sweaters, razor-creased tan pants, and highly polished brown boots that came up over the ankle. For this occasion, however, he'd chosen a nicely tailored blue pinstriped suit, white shirt, and red-and-blue regimental tie.

He kissed my cheek.

"How was the White House?" he asked.

"Pleasant, and impressive. The president was charming. He certainly knew a lot about us and our books."

"A man on top of things," he said, accepting an hors d'oeuvre from a replenished tray passed by a female household staff member.

"Champagne?" I asked, and looked for the man in the white jacket.

He leaned close and whispered, "Any chance of a malt whiskey?"

"Oh, I'm sure that can be arranged," I said, motioning for the server passing the champagne, and asking him for a single malt Scotch. "Of course, madam," he said.

"Is our host here?" George asked, taking in the room.

"I haven't seen Senator Nebel since the White House," I said. "Looks like things run smoothly without him."

"Quite a house," George said.

"To say the least."

As if on cue, Warren Nebel entered the room and quickly made his way to each guest, patting an arm or shoulder, taking women's hands and holding them while he spoke, his smile perpetual, making each person feel as though he or she were the only one there. *The consummate professional politician at work,* I thought.

"Ah, yes, Mrs. Fletcher's special friend, all the way from jolly old London," he said when I introduced him to George. "It's truly a pleasure having you here, Inspector Sutherland. May I call you George?"

"Of course," said George.

"And we'll drop the 'Senator this' and 'Senator that' for the evening," Nebel said.

"That's a deal," said George.

"And we can dispense with the Mrs. Fletcher, too," I added.

"Right you are, Jessica," said Nebel, disengaging and gliding on to the next guest.

George and I ended up in a knot of people, including the Librarian of Congress, Dr. Thomas Lester, who oversaw the library's immense collections, which he proudly pointed out consisted of eighteen million books on more than five hundred miles of bookshelves, twelve million photographs, and almost fifty million manuscripts.

"Astounding," George said, sipping his recently delivered Scotch. "I imagine you have a sizable problem with overdue books."

Dr. Lester laughed heartily, exposing a full mouth of yellowed teeth. "Outright theft is more like it," he said. "Excuse me. I see someone I need a word with."

Another man in our group, Walter Grusin, said to me, "I've been hoping to catch some time with you, Mrs. Fletcher."

"Oh?"

"I'm with the lobbying firm of McCrorry and Castle. You might have heard of us."

"I'm sorry, but I'm afraid I haven't."

I took a stab at judging his age; no older than forty-five. He looked as though he could have been a college football star, solidly built, square faced, and sure of himself. "We represent Sterling Power."

George looked quizzically at me.

"The company that wants to put a large nuclear generating plant near my home," I said, both to acknowledge to Grusin that I understood, and to clue George in.

"You make it sound ominous," Grusin said. "The senator must have gotten to you."

"No," I said, "but it's the topic of considerable conversation in Cabot Cove, as you can imagine."

"Are you a member of the citizen group opposing it?" he asked.

"A member? No. But I have good friends who are, and I've contributed to their cause."

"I'd think a well-known author like you could find better things to do with her money," he said.

I glanced at George, whose expression said he hadn't appreciated the comment any more than I had.

"I'm not against nuclear power," I said, "but there are legitimate questions about locating it there."

"Perfect place for it," Grusin said. "I'd appreciate spending some one-on-one time with you while you're in D.C."

"Are you lobbying me?" I smiled to lighten the question.

"You might say that," he replied. "After all, I am a lobbyist."

"I'm afraid my week is spoken for," I said, hoping I didn't sound too curt.

"Opponents to the plant see it from only one viewpoint, Mrs. Fletcher. I think that if you allow me to outline the alternative perception for you, you might change your mind. We could use someone of your reputation back in Maine to help us present a more accurate picture."

The senator, accompanied by a young man, rejoined us, sparing me any further lobbying by Mr. Grusin. The young man looked like the senator, but lacked his spark. Nebel held a glass filled with ice cubes and liquor. "You haven't met my son," he said to George and me. "Jack

Nebel, say hello to Jessica Fletcher and Inspector Sutherland."

"It's George," George said, shaking Jack's hand.

"Jessica is a famous writer," said Nebel. "She lives near us in Cabot Cove."

"I know," his son replied. "I wrote a review of one of your books for my high school English class."

"Must have been one of my earlier ones," I said. He appeared to be in his early twenties, a handsome young man, slightly overweight, with a softness to his face and sadness in his large brown eyes. I remembered his mother once saying that she worried about him; he never seemed to find his place, drifting from job to job.

"And the inspector—George—is with Scotland Yard," his father said.

Jack Nebel's face brightened. "That must be an exciting place to work," he said.

"It has its moments," George said. "Most of the time it can be bloody dull."

"Like most jobs," Senator Nebel said. "People think being a senator is exciting, but I spend the majority of my days trying to stay awake." He laughed at his comment. "But don't tell that to the voters back home."

"Your secret is safe with me," I said.

Nebel nodded at Walter Grusin. "Don't spend too much time with Walter, Jessica," he said. "You'll end up having a nuclear plant in your backyard."

Grusin had been sober faced when speaking with me. His tone changed with the senator. He slapped Nebel on the back, grinned, and said, "Don't shortchange your constituents, Senator. Have them suffer a blackout and they won't forget it at the polls."

"I think I know my people," Nebel said. "Besides, I still haven't made a final decision on my vote—which, I might add, is why you're still lobbying me."

"That's good to hear," said Grusin. "And by the way, thanks for inviting me tonight. A man who'll invite his enemies to break bread with him is a big man."

"I'm hardly your enemy," Nebel said pleasantly. "While I might not always see your point of view, I recognize that you and your fellow lobbyists are a valuable source of information for any elected official."

"We try our best," said Grusin. He turned to Nebel's son. "How are you, Jack?"

"Okay," Jack said.

"Will your wife be here?" I asked the senator.

"I'm afraid not," he said. "Pat isn't feeling well and begged off. She's in her room, and I encouraged her to rest this evening. She's been on a backbreaking schedule lately, running all over the country promoting her literacy initiative. This week at the Library of Congress is really her idea. I'm just adding some senatorial muscle to it. She'll join us tomorrow, I'm sure."

"Well," I said, "I'm sorry she's not feeling well, but I'm sure the rest will do her a world of good."

It ran through my mind that Patricia Nebel must have really been under the weather to have missed joining her husband at the White House to celebrate what had been her idea and initiative, and to miss the follow-up dinner party in her own home.

A littler later I was subjected to another bit of lobbying by Walter Grusin when George and I found ourselves standing next to him after we'd gone to a bar on which to set our empty glasses.

"May I get you a drink, Mrs. Fletcher?" he asked pleasantly. When I didn't immediately respond, he laughed and said, "No strings attached. No nukes in your backyard. I promise."

"Thank you, no," I said.

"Inspector?"

"Not at the moment, thank you," George said.

Grusin said to the bartender, "Wild Turkey on the rocks with a splash of soda, and a chardonnay." He turned to me. "If you change your mind about finding some time for me this week, I'll be forever grateful."

"I don't think it will be possible," I said. "I have a full schedule."

Nikki Farlow walked up. Grusin took the drinks from the bartender, handing the bourbon to Nikki. She looked surprised. "Thanks," she said, nodded at us, and walked away. Grusin wished George and me a pleasant evening, and followed her.

"Persistent chap," George said.

"I suppose lobbyists have to be," I said.

The sound of a ringing bell announced that dinner was about to be served. Nikki, who seemed to function as the missing lady of the house, motioned for everyone to follow her to a dining room, where a table that comfortably seated forty diners had been elaborately set with gleaming china and silverware. I took note that the four writers in the group had been spread throughout the crowd, and was pleased that George's place card was immediately to my right. The card to my left indicated I'd also be seated next to a Richard Carraway. I hadn't met him earlier or during the cocktail hour, and he was the last person to take his seat at the table. Carraway was a visibly nervous middle-aged man, with a twitch in his left eye. He was short and heavyset; perspiration had wilted his illfitting gray suit and white shirt. I noticed how pale he was. He'd combed disheveled gray hair from low on his right side up over his baldpate.

"A pleasure to meet you," he said, wiping his brow and neck with an already damp handkerchief. "Lots of talk about you coming," he said.

I introduced him to George.

"Scotland Yard, right?" Carraway said. "I heard you'd be coming, too."

"Thanks to Mrs. Fletcher here," George said.

"I take it you work for Senator Nebel," I said.

"In a manner of speaking," Carraway responded. "I work for *her.*" He pointed down the table at Nikki Farlow.

"Quite an impressive lady," I said.

His scowl said he didn't necessarily agree with me. "I'm the Hill's oldest gofer," he said.

"Gofer? The Hill?" George said, laughing. "And I thought we spoke the same language."

"A gofer is an errand boy," Carraway said, "and the Hill is Capitol Hill."

"How long have you been with the senator?" I asked.

"I've been with Nebel since his first term. I handle his

constituent relations, and oversee his staff on the Energy and Commerce Committee. I used to be chief of staff—until he brought *her* in." He nodded in Nikki Farlow's direction.

"Sounds like a challenging job," George said, a hint of his Scottish brogue coming through. "Hardly an errand boy." I sensed he'd said it to appease Carraway, to take the edge off the man's overt agitation.

"Challenging?" Carraway said, guffawing. "It'll kill me." With that he gulped down a large glass of water and looked around for a refill.

Dinner proceeded as most dinners do, with course after course served by the household staff, augmented by uniformed staff who, I learned, were provided by the catering firm hired for the event. We started with crab bisque, went on to a salad topped with crumbled Gorgonzola, and enjoyed a chateaubriand cooked to a perfect pink, garnished with green beans and fingerling potatoes. A different wine accompanied each course, which would have been sufficient. But a number of people at the table, including Senator Nebel, augmented the wine with hard liquor, their glasses refilled by a male member of the caterer's staff who somberly and silently went about the task, circling the table, a bottle in each hand. The East Indian houseman who'd served drinks during the cocktail hour seemed to have disappeared, presumably busy in the kitchen.

Along with rumors of Senator Nebel's straying from his marriage in Washington, there were also claims that he'd become a hard drinker when away from home. Both allegations would not sit well with Maine voters, who tend to value self-discipline and moral integrity. His opponent for a third term had already begun to allude to these weaknesses on the part of our junior senator.

Fueled by the liquor, some members of the party became increasingly boisterous, their voices rising in volume along with their animated telling of tales, jokes, and Washington's latest rumors.

After dishes had been cleared, Nebel tapped a glass with a spoon, stood, and held out his hands in a call for silence. It took a few moments for the last voices to fade away. When they had, and after welcoming everyone, he said, "As you all know, this week devoted to fostering national cultural literacy was not this senator's brainstorm. The credit belongs to my wife, Patricia, who's committed herself to raising an appreciation for literacy, and the arts in general, in this wonderful land of ours."

George leaned close to my ear and whispered, "He's had a tad too much to drink."

I nodded. The effect the drinks had had on Nebel wasn't extreme, but his speech was slightly slurred.

"Of course, kicking off this week was also a good excuse for a party, which I hope you're all enjoying. I want to especially thank Dr. Lester for gracing us with his presence tonight. The Library of Congress is one of our most treasured institutions, and I thank him for his support and leadership in mounting this symbolic and important week."

Many people applauded; a few who'd continued to imbibe gave out with whoops and hollers. The senator's daughter, Christine, sat at her father's end of the massive table. Next to her was a man I'd been told was her fiancé. He appeared to be in his forties; she'd passed her thirtieth birthday but looked like a teenager, small and delicate, and sober faced. The man joined in the applause; she did not, looking very much as though she would rather have been someplace else.

Nebel added to his remarks about the literacy week ahead of us, and concluded by heaping praise on his cook, a Mrs. Martinez—"I might have brought in the caterers, but Carmela planned the menu" (there was applause)—and announcing that dessert and after-dinner drinks would be served on the terrace. Nikki Farlow opened French doors and the sound of a pianist reached our ears.

The brick terrace was almost as large as the dining room. Small individual tables had been set up, and an ice-cream buffet was situated in one corner, a bar in another. The day's heat had dissipated, and a refreshing breeze came up from the river. It was a clear night, the sky filled with twinkling stars surrounding an almost-full moon. The pianist played a medley of showtunes. He'd just segued into "Cheek to Cheek" when George took my hand, placed another at my waist, and we started to dance. I was a little self-conscious because we were the only couple dancing, but I quickly melted into the pleasure of it, ignoring those around us. When the music ended, there was polite applause for our efforts, and we went to the bar, where George ordered a Scotch for himself, sparkling water for me. We found a matching pair of cushioned patio chairs partially shielded from the crowd by small trees in large pots, settled in them, and sighed in concert.

"Your senator lives quite well," George said.

"So different from his persona at home, George. I suppose he campaigns there under the when-in-Rome philosophy. Still, it seems dishonest, doesn't it, to pretend to be one thing for voters, and then turn into something else once you've captured their vote?"

"No different in England, my dear, or anywhere else in the world, I suspect. Have you been introduced to everyone here?"

"Almost everyone, I think. I haven't met his daughter or her fiancé, and there are still a few unfamiliar faces. The other writers were congenial. Senator Nebel seems embroiled in the debate over a nuclear power plant proposed for a site near my hometown."

"So I gathered. Nasty business, politics, being pulled from every direction by special interest groups when legislation is pending."

I nodded and sipped my water. "Enough about politics," I said, placing my hand on his on the arm of his chair. "How is your conference on terrorism going?"

"More politics actually," he replied. "Lots of talk, little substance. Your chaps seem transfixed on your color-coded warning system. The Israelis and Germans take a more pragmatic approach. We Brits seem to think that by debating it in our House of Commons, bin Laden and his thugs will simply fade away. Not much progress, I fear."

We shifted to a recounting of our respective lives since last being together, and were thoroughly engaged in that topic when a voice from behind the potted trees caused us to stop, and to cock our heads in its direction. I was sure the voice belonged to the East Indian servant—his high-pitched voice and singsong cadence were too distinctive to mistake. "You don't threaten me," he said, just loud enough for us to make out his words. "I threaten *you*. I know about you—I have seen you and will tell people."

The words stopped, and we heard two sets of footsteps walk away.

"The chap is obviously angry," George said.

"It certainly sounds that way," I said. I stood and peeked behind the row of potted trees. The East Indian was nowhere in sight, but I did see Jack Nebel, the senator's son, walking away in the direction of the stairs leading to the dock. I looked down. The terrace was paved with a pristine white stone, which provided a background for what appeared to be the partial print of a shoe sole that had evidently stepped in some black substance. Maybe using white stone wasn't such a good idea for the terrace, I thought as I rejoined George. Beautiful, but not especially practical.

We returned to our previous conversation about our lives, but were again interrupted when Christine Nebel's fiancé wandered into our area, a drink in his hand. He seemed startled to see us and said, "Sorry. Don't mean to intrude."

"You're not intruding," I said. "I'm Jessica Fletcher. This is George Sutherland." George stood and shook his hand.

"The Scotland Yard inspector," the man said. "I'm Joe Radisch."

"Please join us," I said.

He pulled up a small white wrought-iron chair.

"You're Christine Nebel's fiancé," I said.

"That's right, for better or for worse."

His comment caused me to pause before saying, "I haven't had the pleasure of meeting her. I'm from Cabot Cove, Maine, and remember seeing the senator's son and daughter with him when he campaigned. But they were younger then. So was I."

Radisch laughed. "I suppose we're all not as young as we used to be. Enjoying this party?"

"Very much," said George. "It's a splendid setting for one."

Radisch slowly shook his head. "Yeah, Christine's father lives well, that's for sure. A senator can make a hell of a lot more than his salary. At least *this* senator."

Was he suggesting that Senator Nebel might be the recipient of outside financial influence? It sounded that way, but it wouldn't have been polite to pursue it. Instead I said, "When do you and Christine plan to marry?" I wasn't particularly interested in his answer, but it was a nonconfrontational question to ask.

He shrugged, downed the remains of his drink, and stood. "There won't be a date if the esteemed Senator Warren Nebel has anything to say about it."

There didn't seem to be an appropriate response.

"You write books," Radisch said to me. "Murder mysteries."

"Yes."

"I've been thinking of writing a book," Radisch said.

"A murder mystery?" George asked.

"Sure," Radisch replied, smiling.

"Who's killed?" George asked lightly.

Radisch extended his hand as though to include everyone on the terrace. "Take your pick," he said. "In Washington, backbiting and double-dealing are daily occurrences, ample motives for murder. Nice meeting both of you. Enjoy the rest of the evening."

When he was out of earshot, George laughed and said, "It doesn't sound as though it's to be a wedding planned in heaven."

I sighed. I'd been to many weddings where one or the other of the involved families wasn't especially happy about their son's or daughter's choice of a mate. Expressing negative thoughts about his future father-in-law to strangers hadn't been especially discreet on Mr. Radisch's part. He was obviously an angry sort of man who probably had few nice things to say about anyone. I wondered what positive qualities he possessed to have attracted Christine Nebel's romantic interest. I often ponder such things when I encounter couples who seem poorly matched, at least on the surface, but learned long ago never to judge why and how men and women end up together. Trying to quantify the chemistry between men and women is as fruitless as attempting to understand the universe itself.

Perhaps it would have been more mannerly for George and me to mix with others rather than stay secluded, but I didn't want to lose the opportunity to spend time with him. Besides, it appeared from our vantage point that no one would particularly miss us. People seemed to have found their own private niches for conversations with those they knew, or had met and with whom they wanted to continue interacting. We kept catching up until I looked at my watch.

"Getting late," I said. "I started out today at the crack of dawn."

"Then we must see that this tired lady gets to bed," he said, standing and stretching against a stiff back. He'd injured it a few years ago when he fell into a moat surrounding the Napa Valley home of a former Hollywood producer and winegrower. That there had been a moat in the first place was bizarre, but reflected our host's peculiarities. It was the last time George and I had been together. We ended up solving the murder of the producer and losing the idyllic vacation we'd planned.

"Know what I'd like to do?" I said.

"What's that?"

"Walk down to the river."

"I thought you were tired."

"I am, but a walk after that big dinner would be welcome."

"The walk back up all those stairs will test us both," he said.

"And I'm sure we're up to the test."

We looked for the senator on our way across the terrace toward the stairs. He was nowhere to be seen. The senator's aide, Richard Carraway, who worked for Nikki Farlow, crossed unsteadily in front of us, a half-consumed drink in his hand, sweat glistening on his round face. George deftly stepped aside to avoid being bumped. "Sorry," Carraway said, continuing on his way.

"I hope he has a designated driver to take him home," I commented.

We stopped to compliment the pianist, who asked if we had any requests.

"Anything by Cole Porter," I said. He immediately launched into "I Love Paris," the catchy rhythm injecting added spring to our steps as we approached the stairs. We stopped short of them as Jack Nebel, perspiring heavily and out of breath, ascended the final few steps. He stopped when he saw us, looked as though he were about to say something, but quickly walked away. His sister, Christine, who stood with her fiancé, Joe Radisch, called out to him, but he ignored her and continued in the direction of the house.

The stairs down to the water were narrow, rickety-looking wooden steps that zigzagged from the terrace— thirty or so steps in one direction to a landing, then thirty or more in a different direction to another landing. We stood at the top and looked down.

"They don't look terribly secure," George said.

"What?" I said.

"I was saying that—"

"I'm sorry," I said. My attention had been diverted by what appeared to be another partial shoe print of the same dark substance I'd noticed behind the potted trees. This one was close to the beginning of the staircase. *Someone is tracking mud all over the terrace,* I thought.

"Coming?" George asked, extending his hand.

"Yes."

We started down, pausing at each landing to take in

the river and surrounding countryside from the varying perspectives the platforms offered. Our way was dimly outlined by solar lamps attached to the edge of every dozen steps, luckily augmented by the glow from the fat moon above.

"He's winking at us," George said.

"Who?"

"The man in the moon."

"Oh, him," I said, laughing. I looked back toward the terrace and the house. The pianist was still playing Cole Porter tunes, and I thought how wonderful it was to be so musically gifted to be able to play, at the drop of a request, wonderful music from composers like Cole Porter and others whose music had brightened Broadway for so many years. My eyes then went to the upper story of the house. Only one window was illuminated, and a woman stood alone silhouetted by the light. She seemed to be peering down at the terrace. Was it Patricia Nebel? I wondered. The picture of her standing there by herself, while festivities played out below her, was profoundly sad. Being the wife of a high-profile United States senator—and being the son or daughter of one—couldn't be easy, and took an especially strong person to deal with the inherent stresses it must create.

We slowly continued our descent, and I realized for the first time that George had been right; climbing back up would be a challenge. The stairs were very steep, and I kept my gaze on the next step down even though George steadied my balance. We reached the last landing before the dock, and were now close enough to hear the river's flow. I walked to the edge of the final set of steps, paused, and gripped George's hand tightly.

"Are you all right?" he asked.

"No," I said. "Look!"

He leaned forward to see what had stopped me. The unmistakable form of a body, shrouded in shadows, was sprawled on the dock, just below the final step. While darkness concealed most of the body, a gray pant leg and black shoe angled across that final step were defined by the light of an adjacent solar lamp.

I followed George down as he went to one knee and felt for a pulse in the neck. He looked up at me, shook his head, and said, "Dead, Jessica. Very dead!"

Chapter Three

W e'd better let someone up there know," George said.

"I'll go," I said.

I started up the steps two at a time, but soon slowed as an ache developed in my legs. By the time I reached the top, I felt as though I were walking on two leaden pipes. The pianist was packing his sheet music into a briefcase, and the staff was in the process of clearing tables and putting away the ice-cream buffet and bar.

I saw through the windows that the guests had retreated inside. I searched for Senator Nebel but didn't see him. Richard Carraway stood near the door leading from the terrace. I went to him and said, "There's been an accident."

His watery eyes said he didn't understand.

"I'm afraid someone has died, falling down the stairs to the dock," I said.

A bolt of understanding crossed his face. "Accident? Somebody's dead?"

"Yes. Who's in charge?"

Carraway looked over his shoulder into the room where the East Indian was again serving drinks. "I don't know," he said. "I'll see if I can find the senator." He walked away before I could say more.

"Hello, Mrs. Fletcher." It was Karl von Miller, the writer of young-adult novels. "Is something wrong?" he asked. "You look pale. Feeling all right?"

"Yes, something is wrong. Someone has fallen down the stairs." I pointed to the ones leading to the dock.

"Oh, my. Seriously hurt?"

"I'm afraid so. In fact—"

Carraway returned with the security guard. "What's this about somebody falling?" the guard asked.

I explained.

He crossed the terrace and paused at the head of the steps. I came up behind him, and looked back to see Carraway and a dozen others approaching.

"Down there," I said. "Inspector Sutherland is with the victim."

"Who?"

"What's happened?" a male voice shouted.

I suffered a moment of shock seeing Senator Nebel cross the terrace in our direction. My first thought seeing the gray pant leg on the stairs was that it might have belonged to him.

I told Nebel what George and I had discovered.

"Get down there," Nebel barked at the guard, who

headed down the stairway, the senator and me on his heels.

"Who is it?" Nebel said to George when we reached the dock.

George, who'd been standing over the body as though shielding it from the embarrassment of being seen in that state, stepped back, allowing the solar lamp to cast muted light on one side of the victim's face.

"Good God," Nebel exclaimed. "Nikki!"

Others had followed us down, and a buzz erupted at the crowd's hearing her name: "It's Nikki?" "She fell?" "Nikki's dead?"

The guard pulled a two-way radio from his belt and said into it, "We have an accident victim at the senator's house. Call nine-one-one. Get some medical help here— and the police."

The senator removed his suit jacket and held it out to George. "Cover her up, for God's sake."

George didn't take the jacket. "Not until the authorities arrive and examine the scene," he said firmly.

" 'The scene'?" Nebel said. "She obviously fell down the stairs. It's an accident. You make it sound as though it's something else."

"Please, Senator," George said, "it's best to not disturb anything."

"This isn't London," Nebel growled. "This is Washington, and this is my home."

George ignored the comments and positioned himself so that he kept anyone else from getting close to Nikki's prone body. The security guard, obviously agreeing with

George's assessment, stepped next to him, another body to shield the deceased from prying eyes.

I walked away from the crowd, giving myself a better, wider view of the scene. I now saw that Nikki had landed on her back. One leg rested against the first step; her arms were splayed. It struck me that if she'd fallen while coming *down* the stairs, she was likely to have landed on her face or side. But that was pure conjecture on my part.

Other questions raced through my mind as I waited for officials to arrive. Why had she left the party and come down the stairs at this time of night? I wasn't thinking of anything untoward, simply wondering what would have motivated her. After all, George and I had decided to do the same thing. I thought back to our descent, and realized taking a misstep would have been easy in relative darkness on the spindly stairs.

I tried to see what her head might have struck during her fall. There didn't appear to be anything protruding from the stairs or from the dock. There was the handrail, of course, and the edges of the steps themselves. She would have had to strike one of those with considerable force to have died from the blow.

But why had she fallen? Was there a loose board that tripped her? Had she been taking medication that dulled her senses? Had she had too much to drink and stumbled down the stairs to her death? I walked to the railing, gripped the top, and gave it a shake. It was loose. Could a weight thrown against it push it out of its foundation? Had Nikki grabbed for the railing? Were there splinters in her hands?

I was deep into those silent questions when the sound of sirens came from the house. Shortly we were joined by two emergency medical technicians, two uniformed officers, and a tall, heavyset black man wearing chino pants, a short-sleeved maroon shirt with WASHINGTON REDSKINS emblazoned on its front, and sneakers. I returned to the knot of people as he introduced himself as Detective Moody of the Fairfax County police, McLean District Station. He instructed the officers to shine light on the scene, which they did with large halogen flashlights. Now Nikki Farlow's face was clearly visible. Her eyes were open wide; so was her mouth, which sagged to one side. A halo of blood surrounded her head.

Moody crouched close to her, examining her face without touching it. He looked up and asked, "Did anyone see this happen?"

There was no response.

He stood slowly, as though the movement caused pain in his legs. "Who discovered the body?" he asked.

"We did," I offered.

"We? You and . . . ?"

"Me and Inspector Sutherland," I said, standing next to George.

"Inspector?" Moody said.

George said, "I'm with Scotland Yard."

Moody looked at me.

"I'm Jessica Fletcher," I said. "Inspector Sutherland and I were guests at Senator Nebel's party. We decided to take a walk down here to the river and—"

"Where is the senator?" Moody asked.

We all looked around, but he was no longer there.

"Must have gone back to the house," Richard Carraway said. "Might I suggest that someone remove Nikki? Seeing her lying there dead like this is upsetting for everyone."

"That's her name?" Moody asked. "Nikki?"

"Nikki Farlow," I offered when no one else did. "She's . . . she was Senator Nebel's chief of staff."

"That's right," Carraway said.

Senator Nebel came bounding down the stairs, followed by his son, Jack. He pushed through those who'd gathered at the scene and announced himself to Detective Moody.

"I recognize you, sir," Moody said, accepting Nebel's outstretched hand, a smile crossing his deeply creviced ebony face. "She worked for you?" he asked, nodding toward the body.

"Yes, my top aide. Invaluable to me."

Moody turned to an officer and requested that he call for a crime-scene investigator, and an evidence technician.

"Crime-scene investigator?" Nebel said, his voice heavy with incredulity. "What crime? The poor thing must have lost her footing and fallen. It's almost happened to me a few times. These stairs are treacherous. I've been meaning to have them replaced since I bought this place. Now I'll never forgive myself for not doing it."

"I'm sorry, Senator, but this is an unexplained death. I have my rules to follow. You're probably right that the lady slipped, fell, and died as a result. But I'm sure you can also understand my need to follow the law, you being a United States senator."

"Looks like I don't have a choice," said Nebel.

"Afraid you don't, sir," Moody said. He addressed the others: "I suggest you all go on back up to the house. But please don't leave. I'd like to have the chance to speak with each of you. Won't take long. Just routine."

He instructed one of the uniformed officers to accompany everyone to the house, adding after the others were out of earshot, "And make sure nobody leaves."

He said to me, "I'd like you and the inspector to stay a few minutes."

When the others were gone, Detective Moody crouched again next to Nikki's body. "No sign of bruising or lacerations on her face," he said to no one in particular. "Must have hit the back of her head. We'll check that out."

"She landed on her back," I said.

Moody stood. "Looks like she did, ma'am. I didn't catch your name."

"Jessica Fletcher."

"Sounds familiar."

"Mrs. Fletcher is a well-known writer of mystery novels," George said.

"Right," said Moody. "I read about you coming to D.C. for some event at the Library of Congress."

"A literacy drive," I said.

"Worthwhile thing," he said. "Wish my kids read more. Not that they don't—read, of course. Just wish they read more. You say you two decided to come down here to the dock? See anybody else do that during the party?"

We shook our heads. I said, "But we really weren't paying attention at the time. Jack Nebel was—"

Moody looked at me and squinted, his expression inviting me to say more.

"That's the senator's son," I said. "When George and I were about to walk down here, he was just coming up the stairs."

The detective grunted.

The remaining uniformed officer had walked away from us and stood at the dock's edge, looking out over the river.

A crime-scene investigator and evidence technician arrived. "What have we got?" Moody was asked.

"Apparent accident," he replied. "But you'd better get the scene on the record."

The CSI motioned for the EMTs to come from where they'd been sitting on pilings a dozen feet from the body. "Give us a few minutes," he said, taking a camera from a shoulder bag and quickly shooting a series of shots of the body from various angles, and wider photos of the dock area and bottom of the stairs. The evidence tech, a young woman with red hair piled high on her head, and with silver fingernails the length of small knives, used a flashlight to search the area surrounding the deceased.

I realized I'd forgotten that George was there. He'd said nothing, content to have lighted his pipe and to quietly puff away a respectful distance from the deceased. He stood next to the Aquasport fishing boat tied to the dock. I joined him.

"Are you all right?" he asked.

"Yes, thank you." I looked over the side of the boat and saw that there was a thin layer of water surrounding the center console; someone's shoes had left footprints in it.

"Oh, my," I said.

"What?"

"Whoever last took this boat out was terribly careless tying it up." I pointed to one of two lines wrapped around cleats on the dock. "They didn't even knot it. It wouldn't take much to have it slip away."

"Good thing you spotted it," he said.

"I've tied up my share of boats in Cabot Cove," I said.

"It appears that you have," he said.

I saw that whoever had last used the Aquasport also hadn't bothered to tip the boat's single outboard engine up out of the water. I moved to the transom at the stern, grabbed the gunwale with one hand to steady myself, and stretched as far as I could with the other to allow my fingertips to touch the engine.

"What are you doing?" George asked in a whisper.

"It's warm," I said in an equally quiet voice. "It's been used recently."

Our attention returned to where the evidence technicians were completing their examination of the scene.

"Anything?" Moody asked the female tech.

"*Nada,*" she replied. "Zip."

"You finished?" Moody asked the CSI.

"Yup."

Moody said to the EMTs, "Turn her over, please."

We watched as an EMT slowly, gently turned Nikki's body over, careful to position her so that her face would not come in contact with a pool of blood that had formed. His colleague placed a white towel beneath her cheek.

"Nasty-looking," Moody said, referring to a four-inch

laceration on the back of her head, running from the mid-line up into the hair on her scalp.

George leaned closer and said, "Hmm."

I turned to him.

"It's vertical," he said in a voice so low I could barely hear him.

Moody heard him and said, "The laceration?"

"Yes," said George. "Hard to see how her fall would have resulted in a vertical wound."

Moody shrugged. "You never can tell how somebody's going to fall."

"True," said George, "but still . . ." He circumvented the body and closely examined the edges of the bottom three stairs, lightly running fingertips over them.

"I hate to disturb you, Inspector," Moody said, "but do you mind telling me what you're doing?" When George started to respond, the detective added, "I know you're some sort of an inspector in England, but if you don't mind, I'd just as soon you not intrude."

"Of course," George said, straightening and smiling. "It's just that the edges of the steps are rounded, worn, not sharp. That's all."

"Yeah, well, I noticed that, too," Moody said defensively. "I also noticed there's no blood on those edges." He stared down at the victim before turning to his officers. "Let's wrap this up," Moody commanded. "Get the body to the ME's office. Until—and unless—the ME says otherwise, I'm calling this an unfortunate accident." He said to us, "Go on up to the house. I'll be there as soon as I can. You know everybody at the party?"

"No," I said. "We met quite a few, but there are some we weren't introduced to."

"Do me a favor and tell everybody to cool it until I get there. You get a roomful of movers and shakers like this, they tend to get nasty."

"We'll do our best," I said, catching a sly smile from George out of the corner of my eye. As we slowly ascended the stairs, the second trip for me, George said, "Remind me, Jessica, to keep my thoughts to myself around Detective Moody."

"Even if your thoughts make sense?" I asked, my legs getting heavy again as we neared the top.

"Perhaps. The detective is right, of course. Unless the medical examiner says otherwise, you can't really question his accident finding."

"But?"

"But if it *was* a fatal accident, it's one of the stranger ones I've come across in my career."

Chapter Four

I wasn't sure what to expect when we arrived back up at the house. I had visions of the serving people continuing to pour drinks, in some cases for people who simply wanted them, in others to mollify guests' anger at being detained. I was right on both counts.

The Ohio congressman I'd seen on C-SPAN, whose name had eventually come to me—James Darzelouski— was ranting to the uniformed officer about being held "captive" as George and I walked through the French doors. "I'm a U.S. congressman, dammit!" he shouted at the young cop, who showed admirable restraint, gently but firmly reminding the congressman that there had been a tragic death, and that he was under orders that no one leave until Detective Moody had had a chance to speak with everyone.

George and I spotted two vacant forest-green leather wing chairs near where the bar continued to function, and took them. I did a fast mental count of people in the room: thirty-four, which according to my rough calculation meant that a half dozen people or so were missing, including Senator Nebel.

The female member of Congress at the party, who represented a district in California, came to where we sat and surprised me by perching on the arm of my chair. "Can you believe it?" she said. She was an attractive short woman with close-cropped coal-black hair and dancing green eyes.

"We haven't met," I said, and made the introductions. Her name was Gail Marshall-Miner.

"I've read a number of your books," she said. "And enjoyed them very much."

"Thank you."

We all looked to where Ohio Congressman Barzelouski continued to berate the officer.

"Someone ought to tell Barzelouski there's no camera on him," she said. "He's always making speeches."

"I'm sure he understands the necessity of staying here," I said.

"That oaf doesn't understand anything," she replied. "He gives Congress a bad name. He's only interested in hearing himself talk or getting attention in the media. Most people in Congress are hardworking and dedicated to the public good. But a few bombastic idiots spoil our reputation and defame the whole house."

I found it odd that the topic of conversation that interested her at the moment was her perception of the United States Congress. The only thing on my mind was the death that had occurred that evening. George sensed what I was thinking, because he changed the subject by asking, "Did you know Ms. Farlow well?"

Ms. Marshall-Miner smiled and replied, "No, I didn't. I don't have much contact with Senator Nebel's office."

But you were one of two members of the House invited to his party, I thought. *Why?*

As though she read my thoughts, she added, "We're personal friends."

"Does he throw parties like this very often?" George asked.

"Warren?" Ms. Marshall-Miner laughed. "He loves to entertain. It's a shame his wife doesn't."

"She's not feeling well, I was told," I said.

"Not unusual," the pretty elected official on the arm of my chair said. "Patricia is . . . How shall I put it? She's delicate. Excuse me. I see they're still serving drinks."

We watched her go to the bar, where she ignored the bartender, took a bottle of whiskey, poured some into a tumbler, added a few ice cubes, and crossed the room to where others had gathered in anticipation of Detective Moody's arrival. He walked in less than a minute later. Barzelouski sidled up to him and proclaimed loudly, "I'm a United States congressman. I have other official appointments this evening, and I'll be damned if I'll have some tinhorn cop tell me I can't keep them."

The room grew quiet as everyone strained to hear what the detective's response would be. Moody, whose height and physical presence were more pronounced in the room's bright lights, stared at the congressman for what seemed an eternity. Finally he said in a low, well-modulated voice, "I suggest you get out of my face, sir. This isn't Congress, and you are not in charge—of anything! Sit down!"

I wanted to applaud, as I was certain others would have done, too, if it hadn't been inappropriate under the circumstances.

"What's your name?" Barzelouski asked, his voice less robust than before.

Moody smiled, pulled a card from the breast pocket of his shirt, and handed it to Barzelouski. "You can take that chair over there," he said, pointing to one against a wall. The congressman paused as though deciding what to do and say next. He answered those questions by saying nothing, and strutting to where Moody had instructed him to go, where he sulked.

"Can I please have your attention?" Moody asked.

"Is she really dead?" a woman asked.

"Yes, ma'am," he replied.

The woman cried, and was comforted by a man I assumed was her husband.

"I won't keep you longer than necessary," Moody told us. "As you know, there's been an unfortunate death down at the dock, a woman who'd been with you at the party. The assumption at this point is that she's the victim of an accident."

" 'Assumption'?" Richard Carraway said. "What else could it be?"

Moody ignored the comment. He said, "I need to have your names, addresses, and phone numbers before you leave. If you're visiting Washington, I'd appreciate knowing where you're staying, and where you'll be going once you leave. I don't know if I'll need to contact any of you again, but that might be necessary—depending upon the outcome of our investigation."

Barzelouski jumped up and said, "Fine. I'm Ohio Congressman James Barzelouski. Here's my card." He tossed it at the feet of Detective Moody and turned toward the door.

"Please detain the congressman," Moody instructed the uniformed officers.

"Get out of my way," Barzelouski snarled at the officer who stepped in his path. The officer was considerably taller and bulkier than the congressman, and stood his ground.

Moody turned his back on them. "Please give the information I requested to the officers," he said. "You're then free to go."

People lined up, many with business cards in their hands. George and I stayed where we were. Because we were visitors to Washington, we felt it appropriate to wait until the city's residents had provided what Moody wanted, and were allowed to leave.

The process took ten minutes. Once the room had cleared out, Moody came to where we sat. "I know you two are visitors," he said. "Where are you staying?"

"The Willard," I said.

"I'm at the Westin Hotel," George said. "I believe it's in the area known as Foggy Bottom."

"Yup, that's where it is," Moody said, noting our responses in a small pad. "Nice places. You live good."

We said nothing.

"Mind staying around a little bit?"

"For what reason?" George asked.

"Well, since it was you who discovered the body, and because you're a famous mystery writer, and you're a Scotland Yard detective, maybe I can learn something. You're never too old to learn."

"We'll be happy to help in any way we can," I said.

"May we go out to the terrace?" George asked, his pipe cradled in his hand. "I'd like to smoke where I won't disturb anyone."

"Go right ahead. I'll find you when I need you."

We excused ourselves from the detective and went to the terrace, where George lit his pipe and took a few satisfied puffs, looking up into the night sky. A breeze ruffled my hair and George moved to my other side to keep the blue smoke from his pipe from drifting in my direction. As we stood there, the medical technicians brought Nikki Farlow's body up from the dock. It wasn't easy for them to navigate the narrow, winding stairs, but they eventually reached the top and passed close to us, disappearing out of view around the corner of the house.

"How sad," I said, "to see an attractive, intelligent woman's life end so suddenly and harshly."

"Had you gotten to know her, Jessica?" George asked.

"No, not at all. I'd had correspondence with her concerning the trip to Washington, and we'd spoken on the phone a few times. We rode together in the limousine here and she told me a little bit about herself. The senator had evidently met her in Chicago during a fund-raising trip and hired her to be his chief of staff. She seemed preoccupied with the details of the evening and the week coming up, so we didn't talk very long."

"You seemed interested in that boat down at the dock. Are you thinking it might have had something to do with her death?"

"I don't know," I said, "but I found it strange that it wasn't tied up properly, and that the engine was left in the water. Whoever had taken it out was either an inexperienced sailor, or was in a very big hurry when he or she brought it back."

"Any ideas who that might have been?"

"Someone involved with the household, I would imagine. Then again, I'm assuming the boat belongs to the house. Perhaps it doesn't. It's possible whoever docked there had nothing to do with Senator Nebel or the party. I'll ask at some point."

George drew on his pipe, his face set in deep thought.

"What are you thinking?" I asked.

He removed the pipe from his lips, sighed deeply, and said, "I wish the detective hadn't so quickly come to the conclusion that this was an accident. I'd feel better if it were being treated as a crime scene until proved otherwise. That's the way we would have handled this in England—assume a crime has been committed until the facts put you in another direction."

"I know what you mean," I said, "but absent any evidence of a crime having taken place, I suppose his protocol dictates that he make the decision he did. Still, he seems to be leaving his options open. After all, he made sure to get the names of everyone who is here, and had some of his people examine the scene as carefully as if he suspected a crime."

A sudden gust of wind blew a speck into my eye. "Ouch," I said.

"What is it?"

"My eye," I said, clapping a hand over it. "There's something in it."

George pulled a fresh handkerchief from his pocket, tucking it into my hand. He leaned close and placed fingertips next to my closed eye. "Maybe we should go back into the house," he said, "and take care of that."

I blinked rapidly and opened my eye, dabbing tears away with his handkerchief. "It feels better now." George's face was close to mine. We looked into each other's eyes. "We probably should go back anyway," I whispered.

"In a minute," he murmured.

"Oh, I'm so sorry. I didn't mean to interrupt anything." The voice came from the direction of the French doors. George and I jumped apart.

"You didn't," George said, clearing his throat. "Mrs. Fletcher had a mote in her eye."

Although most of the exterior lights on that side of the house had been turned off, I could see that the woman was Patricia Nebel, the senator's wife. Dressed in a faded pink sweatshirt and matching sweatpants, she stood and looked left and right, as though unsure what to do or where to go next. I led George to her. "Pat?" I said.

She jerked; my voice had startled her.

"Jessica?"

"Yes. And this is my friend George Sutherland, visiting from London. He's with Scotland Yard."

She offered her hand; it felt cold and clammy, and her grip was weak.

"I'm so glad you're here, Jessica," she said. "I've been looking forward to seeing you ever since Warren said you'd agreed to come for the week."

"It's such a worthwhile endeavor, Pat, and was a lovely evening until—"

"Until this unfortunate thing happened with Nikki," she said, wrapping her arms around herself as though a blast of cold had engulfed her. "I couldn't believe it when Warren told me what happened."

"It must have been a particularly nasty shock for you," George said, "considering you're feeling under the weather."

"Yes, it was," she said. She was a small woman with soft features, which now reflected her mental state. She looked drawn, exhausted. Large black circles defined the area beneath each eye, and there was a slight but discernible tremor in her lips. Were I describing her in a book and had to sum up what I saw in one word, it would have been *frightened*.

She walked away from us, went to the head of the stairs, and looked down, her hands grasping the railing. We came up behind her.

"It happened down there?" she asked.

"Yes," I said. "At the very bottom of the stairs. She evidently lost her footing and fell."

"I suppose she'd been drinking again," Patricia said.

George and I glanced at each other before I said, "I know she was served a glass of something at the party, but I didn't see her drink it."

Patricia's laugh was rueful. "Oh, Nikki enjoyed her liquor."

George offered, "The autopsy and toxological exam will determine how much she'd had to drink."

"I don't know what this will do to the rest of the week," she said, her voice heavy with despair.

"Hopefully," I said, "things can go forward as planned. Are you feeling up to continuing, Pat?"

"I think I'd better be," she said, offering a thin smile. "It's such a worthwhile program, promoting literacy in America. Don't you agree?"

"Oh, yes, I certainly do," I said. "You look cold. Would you like to go back inside?"

"And face all those people?" she said.

"I think most of them are gone by now," I said.

"I know that the detective, whatever his name is, wants to speak with me, but I'd just as soon do it in private."

"Perfectly understandable," said George, tamping down the ashes in the bowl of his pipe and placing it in his jacket pocket.

As we entered the room in which the cocktail portion of the evening had taken place, Detective Moody was in the process of allowing others to leave after having gathered information from them. The only ones left in the room were the Nebels' son, Jack, and daughter, Christine, her fiancé, Joe Radisch, and members of the catering team, who were cleaning up. I was surprised that Senator Nebel wasn't there.

Moody came to where we stood just inside the French doors and said to Patricia, "Feel up to a few minutes with me, Mrs. Nebel?"

"Yes, I suppose so," she said.

Jack Nebel jumped up from a chair and said, "Mother isn't feeling well. Can't this wait?"

"It could," Moody said, "but sometimes it's better to get these things over with right away."

"I agree," Patricia said. "Would you mind coming into another room with me?"

"No, ma'am, not at all," Moody said, and they went through a door leading to another portion of the house.

They'd been gone for only a minute when Senator Nebel made an appearance in the room. He was accompanied by two men, one an older gentleman wearing what might be termed a dark gray power suit, the other, younger man dressed in slacks, a blue button-down shirt, and a pale blue sport jacket.

"Where's that detective?" the senator asked.

"He's gone off to speak with your wife," I replied.

"I told him Mom wasn't feeling well, but he insisted," Jack said angrily.

"Hello, Jack," the older man in the suit said.

"Hi, Mr. Duncan," Jack replied. He said to the younger man, "How are you, Sandy?"

"Okay. I came as soon as I heard."

I suppose the look on my face and George's indicated we were wondering who these newcomers were, and the senator responded, "This is Hal Duncan, my attorney. Sandy Teller is my press aide. I called them as soon as I learned what happened."

I introduced us, wondering why the senator felt the need to immediately call in legal and public-relations help. But, I silently reminded myself, the world of a United States senator was undoubtedly different from the world most of us experience. Having someone die at a senator's home—and a close, trusted aide, to boot—would surely pique the interest of local media. That would explain the need to have someone familiar with handling the press at your side. As for Mr. Duncan, the attorney, I could only speculate that Nebel was concerned at being drawn into the case, perhaps even as a suspect, should the ruling of an accidental fall prove false.

Nebel instructed Duncan and Teller to go to his study, where he'd meet them in a few minutes. He said to me, "May I have a word with you privately?"

I looked at George, whose raised eyebrows indicated he was as interested in why the senator wanted to speak to me as I was.

"Of course," I said.

I followed him through doors to a kitchen that at first glance appeared to be bigger than my entire house back in Cabot Cove. Kitchen help was busy cleaning up under the direction of the household cook, Carmela Martinez, with the East Indian houseman, whose name I didn't know, lending a helping hand.

"Please leave us for a few minutes," Nebel told them.

As they left, two observations came and went. The first

was that Mrs. Martinez was considerably younger than I envisioned she would be. For some reason I expected an older woman. The second observation had to do with the houseman. Don't ask me why, but I noticed that although he wore the same uniform, he'd changed shoes since the cocktail party.

When they were gone, Nebel leaned against a massive granite-topped island, his hands gripping the edge, leaned forward, and said, "I'm about to ask you a very big favor, Mrs. Fletcher."

"It's Jessica," I said.

"Yes, I know. You and Pat are friends. Unfortunately, I never got to spend time with you back home, but Pat thinks so highly of you. She's loved her time with you."

"The feeling is mutual," I said. "You mentioned a favor?"

"I don't know whether I'm entitled to ask you for one. I don't even know if you voted for me. But not only do I know a great deal about you through your books and the publicity surrounding them, but Pat tells me how sensitive and caring you are."

"That's quite a compliment," I said.

"What I'm asking you to do is to help Patricia get through this week."

"Oh? I'm not sure I understand."

"Pat is fragile, Jessica. You might have noticed that. She puts up a good front for my sake, being the wife of a United States senator, and I've always known how difficult it is for her to do that. Believe me, I appreciate it more than she or anyone could know. This week is vitally important to her. She's poured her heart and soul into it, and I intend to do everything I can to ensure that despite the tragedy here tonight, things go forward as planned, and that the week is as much of a success as she and I envisioned."

"That's admirable," I said, "but I still don't understand how I can help."

"Be with her, that's all. She needs a friend like you at a time like this. Support her. I'll do what I can, but this is an insanely busy week in the Senate. She'll need somebody at her side, someone who understands what she's doing, and why she's doing it. I think you're the perfect person. Will you help me?"

I didn't feel I had a choice, and said, "Of course."

He pushed himself off the island, took one of my hands in both of his, smiled, and said, "Thank you, thank you. If I can ever do anything for you, and I mean *anything,* all you have to do is call my private line. Now, you'll have to excuse me." I expected to be handed that private number, but wasn't.

I returned to where George was engaged in conversation with Jack and Christine Nebel, and her fiancé, Joe. We bade them good night and went to where a limousine waited to take us back into downtown Washington. The driver opened the door for us when Detective Moody came from the house. "Mrs. Fletcher," he called, "I didn't want to miss you before you left." He handed me his business card. "If you or the inspector should remember having seen anything, please give me a call. I'd like to stay in touch while you're in Washington."

"Thank you," I said. "We'll call if we have anything that might interest you."

"Good," he said, stepping back as we entered the limo and settled in the rear seat. As we pulled away, I looked back at him and thought that he wanted us to stay in touch with him whether we remembered anything specific or not. I decided I'd do just that.

During the drive, I told George of my kitchen conversation with the senator.

"I'd be flattered," he said.

"Oh, I am," I said, "and I intend to do whatever I can to help his wife get through the week. Still, I wonder at the necessity of it."

"Take it at face value, Jessica, and do your usual outstanding job, no matter what you're called upon to do."

I fell silent.

"What's going through your mind at this moment?" he asked.

"That conversation we overheard."

"The person we heard was angry. No question about that."

"It was the East Indian houseman, I'm sure."

"Speaking with whom?"

"I saw the senator's son, Jack, walking away from the area. I wonder . . ."

"Yes?"

"There was a footprint where they were standing. It appeared that someone had stepped in mud or something dark. I saw the same thing near the top of the stairs."

"You might mention that to the detective next time

you speak with him. What's your schedule like tomorrow?"

"Frankly, I'm not sure. I have it in a folder back at the hotel. What about you?"

"A morning meeting, but free after that. In fact, free for most of the rest of the week. The conference planners scheduled just enough official business for participating organizations to justify sending people from all over the world, and then frees them up to play golf and do whatever else pleases them. So I'm available to help you in any way I can."

I placed my hand on his and squeezed. "I appreciate that, George. I'll just wait to hear from the senator or his people about what they would like me to do with Mrs. Nebel. And I'll let you know where I'll be."

"In the meantime, get a good night's rest. You said you were fagged back at Senator Nebel's house—before we came upon the unfortunate Miss Farlow."

"I know, and the shock of that certainly woke me up, but it's now worn off."

He kissed me lightly on the cheek as we pulled up in front of the Willard, handed me a slip of paper on which he'd written the phone number of his hotel, and encouraged me to stay in touch. "If you're free tomorrow evening, we can have dinner."

"I don't know what the schedule calls for, but I intend to make time for us to have more than one dinner while we're in Washington."

"Sleep tight, my dear."

The driver opened the door and I started to get out.

George touched my shoulder. I turned and said, "Yes?"

"While you're protecting Mrs. Nebel's fragile nature, just remember one thing."

"What's that?"

"It's entirely possible that Ms. Farlow was not the victim of her own clumsiness. If so, it also means that someone with whom we spent time tonight saw to it that she didn't live to come back up those stairs."

I know he didn't mean to plant that grim thought in my mind. Actually the thought had been there all along. But any hope of falling asleep quickly in my suite went by the wayside, and it wasn't until the wee hours of the morning that I finally dozed off.

Chapter Five

Despite my lack of sleep, I awoke surprisingly refreshed. I stayed in bed a few extra minutes after receiving my wake-up call, propped on one elbow and peering out the window into a gray morning. An occasional raindrop hit the windowpane; I was glad I'd thought to pack rain gear along with my extra pair of comfortable walking shoes.

I called room service and ordered tea, an English muffin, and tomato juice, and turned on the TV. The local CNN outlet was in a commercial break. When the anchor came back on the screen, a photo of Nikki Farlow appeared to the right of her head.

"In what appears to have been a tragic accident, Nikki Farlow, Maine Senator Warren Nebel's chief of staff, was found dead last night at the foot of stairs leading down to the senator's dock on the Potomac, presumably from a fall." The television image switched to a view of the dock, obviously taken from a boat on the water. The camera panned up the winding staircase to the bluff on top where the Nebel terrace began. The angle made the stairs look especially precarious. In a voice-over, the anchor continued: "Ms. Farlow, thirty-nine, had been attending a dinner party at the senator's McLean, Virginia, estate with others involved in a literacy campaign championed by the senator's wife, Patricia. Ms. Farlow had worked for Senator Nebel for the past two years, and had a reputation as an especially capable legislative aide. Detective Joe Moody of the Fairfax County police, who was in charge of the scene at the senator's sprawling home, told reporters this morning that while Ms. Farlow's death is considered an unfortunate accident, there is an ongoing investigation into circumstances surrounding her fall and the condition of the staircase. No charges have been made at this time." The image next to the anchor's head now showed a campaign photo of Warren Nebel. "Senator Nebel issued a statement, praising his aide as a 'brilliant administrator whose savvy political observations and tireless efforts on legislation will be sorely missed,' and said he extended his most heartfelt sympathies to her family and friends. In the wake of Ms. Farlow's death, there have been suggestions that there was more between Senator Nebel and his chief of staff than a professional relationship. CNN was unable to confirm those allegations. There has been no further statement from the senator's office."

Her mention of a possible romantic link between the senator and the deceased was dismaying at best, and personally distasteful. There was no need to bring that up, and I now understood Nebel having summoned his press aide to the house shortly after the discovery of the body. Was there any truth to the rumor? Speculation about his extracurricular activities in Washington had floated around Cabot Cove, but nothing concrete had ever surfaced, nor had the name Nikki Farlow been attached to those rumors. One thing was certain: Along with the glory and power of elected office came a parallel scrutiny of your personal life, real and imagined.

The morning newspaper had been delivered along with breakfast, and I scanned it for coverage of Ms. Farlow's death. It was on page four, a short item that stuck to the who, what, why, where, and when of the story, no mention of possible romantic ties between the senator and Nikki.

My suite in the Willard, besides being lavishly decorated in Newport cottage style with white-painted furniture accented with blue lines, plush carpeting, a wall filled with stunning prints, and a glorious view of Washington through windows that actually opened, was also fully equipped as an office away from home. After eating breakfast and showering, I sat at the large desk and went over that day's itinerary. I was faced with a second breakfast at eight-thirty at the Library of Congress, hosted by the Librarian of Congress, Dr. Lester. That would be followed by a tour of the library, and a luncheon in the Senate dining room on Capitol Hill. The afternoon was taken up with another tour, this one of Congress, and then meetings with members of that body involved with the literacy program. Finally, we were to attend a dinner that night at a restaurant on the city's waterfront.

Whew!

I took heart that the note next to the evening's scheduled dinner read, *Optional.* Hopefully George's evening would be flexible and we could hook up for a quiet dinner for two.

I'd hoped to walk to the Library of Congress that morning, but the rain, coupled with the library's distance from the hotel, made me think twice about it. I went to the lobby, where I indulged myself a few minutes to soak in the stunning restoration of this historic beaux arts hotel's public spaces. Its history went back more than 150 years, its rooms, suites, and bars and restaurants stomping grounds for world leaders, generals, poets, office seekers, inventors, and presidents of the United States. After being shuttered for eighteen years, it was restored to its original glory and reopened in 1986 to the delight of Washingtonians, many of whom consider it as important a monument as the Washington and Lincoln memorials.

The friendly doorman hailed a taxi for me, and I soon found myself going through an elaborate security system at the main entrance to the library's newest building, the Madison, one of three housing the LC's huge collection of the world's wisdom. My bag was thoroughly searched, and the jewelry I'd chosen for the day set off the machine. But the guards were friendly, and I was soon waved through. Dr. Lester had mentioned at the party that the security apparatus was as much for keeping bad people with bad things out of the buildings as it was for keeping others from leaving with books not belonging to them. I would find upon leaving that scrutiny of me would be as stringent as when I entered.

I was directed to the first-floor Office of Public Affairs, where we'd been told to congregate, and joined the writers Marsha Jane Grane, Karl von Miller, Bill Littlefield, and others involved with the schedule. Niceties were exchanged, but talk soon turned to the events of the previous night.

"It certainly was a dramatic ending to an otherwise pleasant evening," von Miller said.

"I'm sure the 'drama' of it wasn't lost on you, Jessica," Marsha Jane Grane said.

"I can do without drama of that sort," I said.

"So typically Washington," Littlefield said. "Did you catch CNN this morning? Looks like the senator might have had an interest in Ms. Farlow beyond their official duties."

The public affairs specialist, Eleanor Atherton, a lively middle-aged woman with a bright smile, loudly cleared her throat before saying, "Ladies and gentlemen, might I suggest that we all would be better served if we refrain from discussing what happened last night at the senator's house? It will undoubtedly be a delicate subject around here for the next few days."

" 'Next few days'?" Ms. Grane said, incredulous. "Do rumors evaporate that fast in Washington?"

"There'll be a new and better one to take its place before we know it," von Miller offered.

"I'm afraid you're probably right," the PR woman said, shaking her head. "But in the meantime you know the saying, 'The walls have ears.' We wouldn't want a casual comment to end up in the press."

My colleagues and I glanced over our shoulders and around the room to see if anyone was listening at the door. Ms. Atherton continued: "On a happier note, it's time now for our breakfast with Dr. Lester. I'm sure you'll enjoy it, the food *and* Dr. Lester's remarks. He's delighted you're here."

We were led to an upper floor and ushered into Dr. Lester's spacious office, where the Librarian of Congress awaited our arrival. Floor-to-ceiling bookcases dominated two walls; a large rotating globe stood in front of one of them. There was a television set, a small, round conference table, and two distinct seating areas, three blue leather chairs with wooden arms on the opposite side of the desk, the other a group of tan leather furniture. Sliding glass doors led to a terrace, but the inclement weather precluded enjoying views of the city from that vantage point.

He made a point of greeting each of us personally before suggesting we go to a conference room in which the conference table had been replaced by smaller tables covered with white tablecloths, and set with silverware and dishes bearing the library's official seal. I'd expected to meet Patricia Nebel there that morning, but she was nowhere to be seen. Instead her daughter, Christine, stood just inside the door and assumed her mother's role as hostess. Each table seated six people; Dr. Lester, Christine,

Karl von Miller, Eleanor Atherton, and a woman introduced as Lester's congressional liaison joined me at my table.

"How is your mother feeling?" I asked Christine.

"Not very well," she replied.

"I'm sorry to hear that," I said. "Will she be up to joining us later in the day?"

"I really don't know," she said, turning to Lester and expressing her mother's regret at not being able to attend the breakfast.

"With all the work that wonderful woman has done to launch the literacy initiative," Lester said, "I think she's entitled to some time off." He took in the table and asked, "Don't you agree?"

We unanimously did.

Although we'd been admonished to not bring up the accident at Senator Nebel's home the previous evening, Dr. Lester obviously hadn't received that advice. "I had to leave early, but I heard what happened last night at your house, Christine," he said. "Dreadful. Truly tragic. My condolences to your family."

"Mrs. Fletcher discovered the body," von Miller said between bites of fruit salad.

"It must have been shocking," Lester said.

"Perhaps for most," said von Miller, "but Mrs. Fletcher has a long and distinguished career writing about murder. Perhaps not as much of a shock to her as for us mere mortals."

Everyone looked at me for a response. I shook my head and said, "Writing about murder and coming upon a victim are quite different. Of course," I added, "you're assuming that Miss Farlow was a victim of murder. As far as the police are concerned, it was an unfortunate accident."

"Do you agree with them?" Lester's congressional liaison asked. She was a middle-aged woman with a pretty oval face, whose intense expression indicated that she was vitally interested in everything you thought and said.

"I have no reason to disagree," I replied, attacking my fruit salad.

Von Miller, who seemed pleased that the prohibition on bringing up Nikki Farlow's death had been lifted by Dr. Lester, asked Christine, "Have you talked to your father about the accident, Christine?" His emphasis on the word *accident* made it clear he believed it was anything but an accident.

Nebel's daughter looked for a moment as though she might begin to cry. With her eyes fixed on the table, she said, "I haven't spoken with him about it. Obviously he's extremely upset. Nikki was one of his closest aides."

Ms. Atherton smoothly and quickly changed the subject by suggesting to her boss, the Librarian of Congress, that he might give everyone at the table a hint at what that morning's tour would encompass. Lester, delighted to pick up the conversational baton, went through a long and detailed explanation of the areas we'd be taken to within the vast LC complex. He was a man clearly in love with his job as overseer of the world's largest repository of information, and spoke with great animation about the various divisions of the library and their importance as a resource for researchers. "We have material in almost five hundred languages," he proudly said, "and we have offices in Rio, Cairo, New Delhi, and numerous other countries throughout the world, including acquisition offices in Moscow and Tokyo. You probably know that the library was founded by Thomas Jefferson more than one hundred and fifty years ago. It's critically important that our work continue for the sake of mankind and its continuing quest for knowledge, and an understanding not only of where we came from, but also of what possibilities exist for the future." He smiled and added, "Of course, that takes money. The term *librarian* is a misnomer for me, I'm afraid. I spend most of my time not with historic books but going over the library's financial books with Congress. With four thousand employees to pay, the upkeep on the three buildings, and trying to catalog electronically more than a million items in the back rooms that haven't even been examined yet, it takes a lot of money."

"Fortunately, there are members of Congress who believe in what we do and fight for funding every year," said his PR woman. "Senator Nebel is certainly one of those."

Lester looked at Christine and said, "Yes, you can be proud of the fight your father wages every year to see to it that we have the necessary funds to continue our work."

"Dad believes in it," Christine said quietly. "I know that for certain."

When breakfast was finished and the tables had been cleared, Lester went to the end of the room and gave a short speech, which sounded more like a pitch for funds than a simple welcoming address. At the conclusion we headed off on our tour, which took an hour and ended up in the main reading room. Our guide, Ms. Atherton, who invited us to call her Eleanor, pointed up to a domed ceiling, 160 feet high; a female figure in its cupola represented human understanding, she told us. Surrounding the figure were a dozen other paintings saluting those countries that had contributed most to the development of Western civilization.

"This room reopened in 1991," she said, "after being closed for more than three years while renovations took place. Every reader desk is now wired for computers, and this soundproof carpeting was installed to cut down on any distracting noise." She pointed up to glassed-in balconies overlooking the room. "We enclosed those areas to cut down even more on unnecessary noise."

I took in the people in the room. Most of the desks were occupied by serious-looking men and women hunched over books they'd checked out from the main desk, or typing into their laptops. I noticed one man wearing a black cape who sat at one of the desks, a tall pile of telephone directories next to him, and wondered why he simply didn't call Information to come up with the phone number he was seeking. Eleanor noticed my interest in him and whispered in my ear, "He's here every day. He believes that someone placed a curse on him years ago, and he's going through every telephone book from around the world to find the name of that person."

My eyes went up. "Oh," I said.

She pointed to a woman occupying a desk at the other side of the room, and said, "We call her the bride of Christ.

She believes she was married to Christ, and is systematically going through every Bible, in every language, to prove her point." She added, "While a few eccentrics add color to our day, the overwhelming majority of people using the library's services are legitimate scholars researching important works, which will contribute to the world's knowledge base."

It had stopped raining during the time we spent touring the Library of Congress, and we were able to walk the short distance to Capitol Hill rather than take the vehicles that waited for us outside the library. It wasn't my first visit to the Capitol building. Our senior senator from Maine, Marjorie Hale, with whom I'd struck up a semblance of a relationship, had hosted me there on two previous occasions, arranging for a personal tour, and gaining me access to the gallery in the Senate chamber, where I was privileged to sit through spirited debate on issues of national concern. As we approached the building this morning, feelings of awe and respect pulsated through me. Its baroque dome with a nineteen-foot bronze statue of Freedom—occasionally called *Armed Freedom* because the female figure dressed in flowing drapery held in her right hand a sheathed sword and in her left a shield—was a beacon of democracy, and the model for most of our statehouses around the country.

Although we were part of an official entourage, we were subjected to stringent security as we entered the building, where we were greeted by Senator Nebel's press secretary, Sandy Teller. We followed him into Statuary Hall, formerly the chamber for the House of Representatives, now a showplace for statues of two notables from each of the states. Next on our tour was the Old Senate Chamber, where such great speakers as Calhoun, Clay, and Webster left their oratorical mark on the nation; it eventually became the home of the Supreme Court before that august body moved to its own building.

The tour lasted an hour and a half, and by the time we were taken to the Senate dining room, I was thankful I'd remembered to pack comfortable walking shoes. A long table had been set in one end of the room for our group, and we looked for our names on place cards before taking our seats. Christine Nebel had disappeared during the tour, her role now taken by Teller, whose smiles seemed more forced and disingenuous than on the previous night.

We'd no sooner been seated when Senator Nebel entered the room, stopping at several tables to greet Senate colleagues. When he finally reached our table, he smiled broadly and announced, "In honor of your visit, this has been declared Maine Day in the dining room. They often designate days for different states featuring food from those places. I haven't seen the menu, but I'm sure there will be at least one lobster dish on it.

"Unlike with our British friends, liquor isn't served here or in any of the official dining rooms of the Capitol, so you'll have to content yourselves with soft drinks and Virgin Marys. In the Houses of Parliament in London, there are bars to which members retire for a little libation after debating weighty issues on the floor. Seems civilized to me." We laughed along with him.

A chair had been left available for the senator, but he told us that he wouldn't be able to stay for lunch. He wished us all a good day, thanked us for our efforts on behalf of the literacy program, came around behind Teller, placed an envelope in front of him, and left, slapping backs and shaking hands on his way out.

Teller, who sat next to me, frowned as he opened the envelope and read the note it contained. He took in the table, and when he saw that everyone was engaged in conversation, he turned and handed the note to me.

Dear Jessica Fletcher:

I hate to disrupt your day, but I would be most appreciative if you would come to my office following lunch. Sandy Teller will escort you.

It was signed, *Warren.*

I looked at Teller, who raised his eyebrows and shrugged.

"Do you have any idea what this is about?" I asked him in a low voice.

"About last night, Mrs. Fletcher."

"What about last night?"

He checked to make sure no one was listening, leaned over, and whispered in my ear, "The senator is really under the gun, Mrs. Fletcher. I know he asked you for a favor last night to help Mrs. Nebel through the ordeal of this week, and what happened at the house with Nikki Farlow."

As lunch was served, I went through an internal debate. I didn't want to become entwined in any problems Senator Nebel and his wife might be having, particularly since it now involved the death of one of his closest aides on the Hill. It had been my bad luck—and George Sutherland's, too—to have come upon her body. On the one hand, I liked Pat Nebel and felt a great deal of sympathy for her. Clearly she wasn't well, and I've not been one to turn my back on someone in need of help. On the other hand, the week promised to be strenuous and busy enough without taking on the added burden of playing what appeared to be nursemaid to her. What to do? I could, at least, go to the senator's office with Mr. Teller and see what he was asking of me, and I could make my decision then.

At the conclusion of lunch—and without offering an explanation to the rest of the group—Teller led me from the dining room, back through the splendid, baronial halls of the Capitol, and down to the basement, where an underground rail system connected that building with all the office buildings housing members of the House and Senate. We rode one of the cars to the Dirksen Building, took an elevator up, and were soon standing in the reception area of Senator Nebel's office. Teller opened the door to the senator's private quarters and I heard him say, "Mrs. Fletcher's here."

Teller closed the door behind me as he left. Nebel, in shirtsleeves, was seated behind a broad desk on which tall piles of paper were neatly arranged. He pulled off half-glasses, rubbed his eyes, shook his head, stood, and came around the desk to shake my hand. "Thank you so much for coming, Jessica. I know this is an intrusion into your week."

"You said last night you wanted me to assist Pat, and I assume that's what this is about," I said.

"Yes, it is. Please, take a seat."

I sat in one of a pair of oversize red leather chairs across the desk from where he resumed his seat. He rested his elbows on the desk and made a tent with his fingers, which he placed under his chin. "I'll cut to the chase, Jessica. This dreadful accident that happened last night has created all sorts of problems for me, and I'm afraid I'm going to have to be focusing all my attention to solving them. In the meantime, there is the literacy program to go forward with, and Senate business as usual, particularly with a vote coming up on the nuclear power plant proposed for outside Cabot Cove. In a sense, I suppose I'm asking you to temporarily join my staff." He shrugged. "It's only for a week."

"And my duties would be?" I asked.

"Be a buddy to Patricia. I just don't have the time to devote to her, and I feel lousy about that. She hasn't made many friends here in Washington. Hell, that's an understatement. It was like pulling teeth to get her to spend any time here at all. She's very shy—almost reclusive, I might say. She loves our home back in Maine, working in her garden, cooking in the kitchen. I've tried to convince her that a U.S. senator needs a full-time wife here. It's expected." He sounded petulant, then thought better of his tone. "Well, it certainly would be helpful. But that's not the way she is. At any rate, because she loves reading so much—God, she must go through five or six books a week—she agreed to come down here with me to launch this literacy initiative, and has done a bang-up job. But not feeling well, coupled with Nikki's death, has really put a strain on her that I'm afraid she's capable of breaking under. I'm not asking you to do this full-time, Jessica, just for the next few days until things settle down."

I wondered if by "settling down" he meant the press scrutiny that had already begun to develop over Nikki Farlow's death, and the rumor that his relationship with her might have been more intimate, and less proper, than what was expected of a senator and his aide. I didn't ask.

"What do you want me to do?" I asked.

Nebel stared down at his desk for a moment, then looked up, his eyes pleading. "Pat is resting today at home. I have a car waiting downstairs to take you there. Will you go spend the afternoon with her? You know, be a girl-friend of sorts, chat about Cabot Cove and Maine, and all the things she loves. I think it would do her a world of good, a lot better than any doctor or shrink could."

I thought for a moment before saying, "Yes, I suppose I can do that. I do want to clear my evening, however, to have dinner with my friend George Sutherland. You met him at your house."

Nebel brightened. "Ah, yes, the Scotland Yard inspec-tor. Splendid chap. I'd like to find some time with him, myself. I'm a bit of an Anglophile, always loved my trips to London and the Cotswolds. You'll do it then?"

I nodded. "Yes, I'll do it."

"Wonderful." He got up from his chair, came around the desk, and clasped my hand in both of his. "I owe you, Jessica, and I don't forget what I owe my friends. You name it here in Washington, it's yours. All you have to do is call me on my private line."

If I intended to take him up on the offer, I might have asked for his private number. I didn't.

When I left Nebel's office, Sandy Teller was standing immediately outside the door with Richard Carraway, the senatorial aide I'd met at dinner last night. We exchanged brief greetings before Teller accompanied me to the front entrance of the Dirksen Building at First and C streets, where a black Town Car was waiting, its engine running. Teller opened the back door for me. When I was settled with my seatbelt on, he leaned in and said, "I assure you the senator is deeply grateful for this, Mrs. Fletcher. Deeply grateful."

With that he shut the door, and the driver, a large man with a shaved head who hadn't yet acknowledged my presence, pulled away from the curb.

The air in the car was frigid. I leaned forward.

"Good afternoon," I said. "Would you mind lowering the air-conditioning? It's very cold back here."

He didn't reply, but reached out and with thick fingers turned a dial to raise the temperature.

"Thank you," I said, sitting back in the black leather seat. I shivered and rubbed my arms to warm them up. But I wasn't sure if the chill that ran through me was from the cold or from the eerie feeling I had that I was unwittingly being thrown into a potentially risky situation. Although I had nothing tangible to base it on, I couldn't shake the notion that a paraphrased line from *Hamlet* was appropriate: Although this wasn't Denmark, something was decidedly rotten here, and I didn't doubt as we headed for McLean, Virginia, that I was about to get closer to the odor.

Chapter Six

Senator Nebel must have called ahead, because the security guard waved us right through. We pulled up in front of the house; the driver came around to my side and opened the door.

"Thank you for turning down the air-conditioning," I said as I got out.

"Yes, ma'am."

I watched him pull away, and wondered what arrangements would be made for me to leave later in the day. I hadn't called George to see whether he was free for dinner, and made a mental note to do that as soon as possible.

I knocked. The door was opened by the East Indian who'd spent the previous evening serving drinks, and whose angry voice I had heard arguing with someone behind the potted trees.

"I believe Mrs. Nebel is expecting me," I said.

"She is resting," he replied, "but she told me you

would be coming. Please, madam, come inside and make yourself comfortable."

He led me to the room in which the cocktail portion of the previous evening had taken place.

"Might I get you something to drink, madam?" he asked.

"A cup of tea would be nice, if it isn't too much trouble."

"Of course, madam," he said, and left the room.

I went to the wall of windows overlooking the terrace and the Potomac and was flooded with thoughts of the dinner party and its unfortunate conclusion. The entire evening played out in my mind—the arrival at the house and my surprise at how opulent it was; the conversations during cocktails; the dinner itself and the individuals involved. And, of course, the dessert on the terrace and the fateful trip George and I had taken down the rickety wooden stairs.

I was deep into those thoughts when the serving man returned carrying a tray on which sat a teapot, a cup, silverware, a pitcher of cream, a small dish of lemon slices, a plate containing three wafer-thin cookies, and a bowl in which sugar had been perfectly leveled. He placed it on a table near the window. "Anything else, madam?" he asked, sliding out a chair.

"No, thank you. This is just lovely. I'm sorry, but I don't believe we've ever exchanged names. I'm Jessica Fletcher. I'm a friend of Mrs. Nebel's."

"Yes, madam. I know who you are. My name is Jardine."

Unlike my first exposure to him when he was dressed in white jacket, white shirt, black trousers, and tie, this day he was considerably more casual—black T-shirt, chino pants, and deck shoes.

"Have you worked for the Nebels for a long time?" I asked, taking the chair he held for me.

"Oh, yes, madam, for more than four years now."

"Did you know Ms. Farlow well?" I asked.

"Ms. Nikki visited the house often," he said, his expression indicating that he weighed how much he should tell me. "She is . . . she was a very important person for Senator Nebel."

"Yes, I understand that. Have the police been back to the house?"

"No, madam, I have not seen any policemen. Excuse me, please. I have chores to do."

"Of course," I said. "Thank you for the tea."

I'd debated asking him whether he'd had an argument the previous night, perhaps with Jack Nebel, but decided to save it for another time.

He was almost out of the room when I called after him, "Jardine, do you know when Mrs. Nebel will finish her nap?"

"No, madam, but I will check on her and let you know."

The tea was delicious, and I found myself relaxing in the comfortable chair. But my attention kept being drawn to the outdoors and the head of the stairs leading down to the dock. I got up, opened the door to the terrace, and stepped outside. The sky was a menacing gray punctuated with black clouds, but no rain fell. I went to the stairs and looked down; going down them at night, even with the dim light provided by the solar lamps, posed a distinct threat of accident.

I almost turned back to the house, but took the first few steps down the stairs, as though operating on automatic pilot. I held the railing tight as I navigated each section of the stairway, pausing at the various landings to look back and down before continuing my descent. A dozen steps from the dock I saw a black smear on one of them similar to what I'd seen on the terrace. And when I reached the dock, another such blemish on the gray, weathered wood caught my attention.

The Aquasport was tied to the dock. Had someone taken the boat during the party, and hastily returned it to the dock? I wondered. Two crews from one of the many universities in Washington were practicing on the river, and I enjoyed watching the smooth, synchronized movement of their sculls through the river's dark waters. My interest in them was short-lived, however. I looked down at the telltale red stain on the dock—Nikki Farlow's blood. It didn't appear as though anyone had even attempted to clean it up, which I found strange, and unquestionably insensitive.

I stepped around it and did what I'd done the previous night: took in that area from a wider vantage point. It had occurred to me during the time the police were there that it was unusual that she'd landed on her back. But then I realized what a false assumption I'd made; that she had been coming *down* the stairs. It was possible that she had started up and had fallen backward.

That prompted another question. I was no expert on people falling down stairs to their death, but my assumption was that most falls occurred when people were descending, not ascending. Of course, if Patricia Nebel had been right, that Nikki Farlow was more than a casual social drinker, it was easier to accept the scenario that she'd started up the stairs, had become light-headed, and toppled back.

I returned to the stairs and examined the edges of the first three steps, as George had done last night. He was right: The edges of the steps were rounded, perhaps deliberately by whoever had built them, or naturally worn away with age. They were clean; there wasn't a trace of blood to be found on them, although I was aware that you couldn't always trust your eyesight to pick up minuscule droplets of blood, particularly on a surface as porous as the wood from which the steps had been made. Should Detective Moody decide to treat it as a potential crime scene, the use of various chemicals, including Luminol, would determine whether blood was present that the naked eye was incapable of seeing.

As I straightened up from the crouch I had assumed to look at the edges of the steps, my hypothesis that Nikki had fallen while beginning to go up the stairs made more sense than ever. If she hadn't hit her head on the edge of the steps, had the laceration been caused by her head striking the flat surface of the dock?

I remembered George making a comment that the laceration of the back of her head was vertical. I accepted that his observation was important, although I wasn't versed enough in forensic medicine to question what sort of laceration would occur when the back of a head hits a solid object. But it did strike me as strange that a laceration of any kind, vertical or horizontal, would have resulted from that fall. I could certainly understand it if the impact of Nikki's head on the wood had fractured her skull and produced internal bleeding. But a gash like the one we saw just didn't make sense.

I positioned myself at the foot of the stairs, careful to not step on the bloodstain, narrowed my eyes, and tried to envision what had happened.

Nikki had come down to the dock for some unknown reason. When she started back up the stairs, she lost her balance because of alcohol or drugs, couldn't catch the railing with her hand in time, and fell backward, landing on the dock. But the idea that had propelled me down the stairs in the first place that afternoon took hold once again, and my arm involuntarily rose above my head. If someone had used a weapon and struck Nikki in the back of the head as she was going up, she might have toppled backward. But it was more likely she would have pitched forward. Then again, if she were struck while still standing on the dock and tried to escape up the stairs, that, too, could explain both her falling on her back as well as the vertical gash in her head. If that scenario held true, her death was no accident.

Nikki Farlow had been murdered.

I backed away and looked down at the dock beneath my feet. Small spots of discoloration on the dock's weathered wood, decidedly different from the larger black stains caused by a shoe, caught my attention. I backed away a few paces more, went to my knees, and lowered my face to within inches of what I'd seen. I'd once attended a forensic seminar on blood spatter with Dr. Seth Hazlitt, my dear friend from Cabot Cove. He'd spent two years as the town's medical examiner, and had invited me to attend the seminar with him. I tried to remember what I'd learned at the time. The tiny discolorations could have been anything—gasoline, oil, coffee, a soft drink. It could also have been blood. If a weapon of some sort had been used to hit someone in the head, its backward motion after the blow had been struck would usually result in what was called cast-off spatter, blood from the victim's head flying off the end of the weapon. The spots I was examining were pretty much where such cast-off spatters would have occurred, assuming, of course, that my thesis was correct.

I again leaned close to the spots, and was in that position when the sound of footsteps on the stairs caused me to look up. Approaching me was Jack Nebel, the senator's son.

"Mrs. Fletcher?" he said, pausing at the landing just above me.

"Hello," I said, feeling foolish and getting to my feet.

"What are you doing here?" he asked.

"Just looking around, I guess."

He joined me on the dock. "Mother is looking for you," he said.

"She was taking a nap when I arrived," I said. "If she's awake, I'll go right up."

He didn't move from his position at the foot of the stairs, which blocked my access to them.

"Why were you down on your knees like that?" he asked.

He appeared larger than I'd remembered him from the party. He wore jeans, white sneakers, and a blue T-shirt on which was what I assumed was a picture of a rock band.

"Just my natural curiosity," I replied, adding a chuckle.

"Why would you be curious about where an accident took place?" he said.

"I really can't explain it," I said, also thinking that I didn't have any need to. "I suppose because it was me and my friend who discovered the body, I have a need to revisit the scene."

"To make more of it than it really is?"

"What do you mean?"

"It was an accident, Mrs. Fletcher. The police said it was an accident, and my dad agrees. He says that maybe because you write murder mysteries, you view everything as something sinister."

"I assure you—and your father—that's not the case," I said, hoping I wasn't sounding too defensive. "I think I'd better get up and see your mother. I know she hasn't been feeling well, and—"

He stepped aside to allow me to move past him.

I stayed where I was and said, "I think you have a skewed notion of me and why I'm here," I said. "I know that the initial finding was that she died accidentally, but I'm not sure that will hold up. And I assure you it's not because I write murder mysteries that I'm thinking that."

Before he could respond I said, "Is the boat yours, Jack?"

"It's a family boat. I use it most."

"I noticed that it might have been used while the party was going on. Did you take it out for a spin?"

"No," was accompanied by a shrug.

"Well," I said, "whoever did didn't know a lot about boats."

"Why do you say that?"

"This person, whoever it was, left the outboard engine in the water, and didn't even bother to tie the line to the cleat."

"That wouldn't be me," he said. "I've taken courses from the coast guard. I know lots about boats."

"The Aquasport is a lovely boat, very popular in Cabot Cove."

"I like it," he said.

It occurred to me as I stood there that the boat must have been taken during dinner, and before the guests went to the patio, where its engine noise could have been heard. I tried to remember whether I'd seen Jack during dinner but had no specific memory one way or the other.

"Mind if I go aboard?" I asked.

"Be my guest."

I didn't miss the irony in his voice.

A motorboat had just passed at excessive speed, causing the Aquasport to bob wildly. I waited until its movement had subsided before carefully stepping onto the boat and going to the center console, where the controls were located. Jack came aboard behind me. I drew a deep breath and sighed. "There's something uplifting just being on a boat in the water," I said. I turned to him. "Do you feel that way, Jack?"

"I like it," he said.

I looked down and saw the key in the ignition.

"Someone forgot the key," I said.

"I left it there," he said. "I always do."

"You're not concerned about someone stealing it?"

"Nah. Nobody comes down here except me and some of the others in the house."

The practice of leaving a key in the ignition didn't seem especially prudent to me, but I didn't press it. We leave keys in ignitions and doors all the time in Cabot Cove, although a recent series of house burglaries had made that habit less frequent.

"I barely got to meet your sister," I said, keeping things casual. "I did have a chance to speak with her fiancé. Joe Radisch, is it?"

"Him!"

"What does he do for a living?" I asked.

"Nobody really knows."

"Oh? Sort of a mystery man?"

"He claims he's in real estate, but that doesn't check out."

"Ah," I said. "Your dad had him checked out."

"Nikki did."

"Nikki? Why would she do that?"

He hesitated before answering. "Nikki ran things, including my father. Joe's okay, but Nikki didn't like him." He guffawed. "That's an understatement. She hated him, and convinced my father Joe wasn't good for Christine. She should have minded her own business."

I digested what he'd said before replying, "She did seem very much like a take-charge woman."

"That's an understatement. Look, I have to leave, and Mom's waiting for you."

"Of course. Thanks for letting me spend a few minutes at the wheel." I laughed. "Maybe you'll take me for a spin before I leave Washington."

"Sure."

I allowed him to step from the boat onto the dock before I did. During those few seconds, my attention went to his shoes. He wore white sneakers. Judging from the pattern of the sole that was discernible, the partial shoe prints I'd seen on the terrace and on the stairs had been made by a shoe with a smooth sole. As I took steps to leave the Aquasport, my eye went to where the outboard Evinrude engine was mounted to the transom. It had an obvious slight oil leak; a puddle of oil had formed beneath it in the boat and had spread slightly beyond.

"Jack," I said.

He'd started up the steps and turned at my voice.

"Do you know you have an oil leak in the engine?"

"No," he said. "I'll take a look later."

When I reached the top of the stairs, Pat Nebel stood in the expanse of downstairs windows overlooking the terrace. She waved, and I returned it. She looked considerably better than she had the night before. She'd applied makeup and had dressed in a pastel pantsuit. She crossed the room when I entered and gave me a hug. "Jessica, how good to see you again."

"You look rested, Pat," I said, standing back and taking her in. "Feeling better?"

She nodded, but the smile that had been there when I entered the house quickly disappeared.

"I see Jardine served you tea," she said, indicating the tray on the table with its empty cup.

"Yes. It hit the spot."

She looked out the window at the wooden stairs leading to the dock, closed her eyes tightly, opened them, slowly shook her head and said, "I still can't believe what happened to Nikki. Let's go to another room, Jess. Being here reminds me of what happened."

I followed her into the recesses of the house to a small, tastefully furnished room at the opposite end. I would have assumed it was a guest room, but a desk, computer, and file cabinets said otherwise.

"My home office," she said lightly. "Warren and I have his-and-hers offices. Why I need an office here is beyond me. I spend so little time in Washington that it seems a waste to have a room devoted to me."

"But, as a senator's wife, I'm sure you have lots of responsibilities," I offered, not sure I was right, but saying what I thought was appropriate.

"More tea?" was her response.

"Thank you, no."

We sat next to each other on a floral love seat. A few moments of silence seemed longer than that. Finally she said, "Jardine said you were down at the dock."

"Yes, I was."

"How could you? I mean, what would cause you to go back to where that dreadful accident occurred?"

"Your son asked me the same question," I said. "I don't know, Pat, just my curiosity genes coming to the fore."

"It *was* an accident, wasn't it?" she asked, searching my eyes for insight.

"That's what the police say, although the detective did leave his options open. They'll be doing tests on Ms. Farlow to see whether alcohol or drugs might have played a role in her death."

"You're being evasive, Jess," she said, smiling to soften the accusation.

"I suppose I am," I replied. I patted her arm. "But let's talk about more pleasant things. I assume you're ready to take part in the Literacy Week activities, judging from the way you look."

"I decided I'd better, considering it was my idea. I know Warren is up to his neck with Senate business, and I hate to stick Christine or others with my responsibilities. How has it been going so far?"

"Just fine," I replied. "We had a lovely breakfast at the Library of Congress and a tour, and then enjoyed lunch in the Senate dining room. They declared it Maine Day in our honor, which I thought was rather nice. The lobster salad was divine."

"I'm glad to hear it. Warren called and said you'd be coming here this afternoon, I assume to keep an eye on me. I hate to see your enjoyment of the day interrupted for such a silly reason."

"Not silly at all," I said. "Warren is concerned about

you and thought we both might enjoy getting together for an afternoon. I think he suggested we engage in 'girl talk.' " We both laughed. "Nothing wrong with that."

Her brow furrowed and her lips tightened as she looked away from me. When she turned in my direction, she said, "You've heard the rumors about Warren and Nikki, I'm sure."

If this represented girl talk, I could easily have done without it. I acknowledged I'd seen a report on television hinting at it.

"It's true," she said flatly.

Now the silence was on my end.

"If you'd rather not talk about it, I'll—"

"No, Pat, go ahead. That's what friends are for—and I am your friend."

"They'd been having an affair for the past year."

"Has Warren acknowledged it?" I asked.

"Oh, no. When I confronted him with it he became very angry. He has quite a temper, you know."

"No, I didn't know. I suppose politicians are good at keeping tempers in check, at least as far as the voting public is concerned."

"Exactly. He accused me of being paranoid, of seeing women in his life who aren't there. Maybe it's my fault, not being the sort of wife a United States senator deserves. I don't like politics, Jess, and have tried to stay away from it. Maybe if I'd spent more time with Warren here in Washington, such things wouldn't happen."

"Nonsense," I said, thinking that he'd once been caught in the midst of an affair with an aide back in

Maine. "Don't you dare blame yourself for Warren's behavior."

"You're right, of course, and I try not to. The problem is . . ."

I cocked my head and waited for her to continue.

"The problem is, Jess, that Nikki turned out not to be the most honorable of mistresses—if there is such a thing."

"What do you mean?"

She replied without hesitating: "Nikki has been blackmailing Warren about their affair."

I sat back and rearranged myself on the love seat. Being told about Warren's infidelities by his wife was bad enough, but this added an entire new dimension to the picture.

"How do you know this, Pat?"

"I'm not a snoop, Jess, and I've never deliberately pried into Warren's life outside the home. But I ended up privy to a conversation between Warren and his attorney, Hal Duncan."

"I met him briefly last night," I said.

"They were talking about how to handle the situation with Nikki. She was threatening that she would ruin his run for a third term."

"Are you sure you interpreted the conversation correctly?" I asked.

"Oh, yes, I know what I heard. They stopped the conversation the moment they saw me. They acted so guilty."

I asked, "Did Nikki give Warren an ultimatum in terms of when the money had to be paid?"

"Not that I'm aware of, although if she wanted to ruin his political career, she'd have to do it pretty quick."

I didn't say what I was thinking at the moment, that if Nikki Farlow's death had been an act of murder, the husband of the woman sitting next to me, Senator Warren Nebel, certainly had a motive to kill. But I didn't have to say it, because Patricia did.

"I think Warren killed Nikki," she said.

Chapter Seven

An hour later Pat Nebel walked me to the front door of her home. It had been a wrenching time for me, and I'm sure it wasn't easy for her to talk openly about the state of her marriage. I'd listened patiently as she talked of the trials and tribulations of being the wife of a United States senator, and there were times when I wondered whether I should suggest a change in subject. But she seemed anxious to confide in me, and I felt an obligation to be a good and sensitive listener. I couldn't help but wonder whether Senator Nebel would have been so anxious for me to spend time with his wife if he knew what she was thinking, and had said to me.

At the end of the hour, I said I needed to get back to my hotel in preparation for meeting my friend George Sutherland for dinner that night.

"The Scotland Yard inspector," she said.

"Yes."

"Ironic, isn't it, Jess, that a Scotland Yard inspector would be here the same evening that a murder occurred?"

"Pat, I must remind you that no one has said that Nikki Farlow was murdered."

My words, I knew, fell on deaf ears. It was upsetting enough that she was convinced that Nikki had been murdered. What was worse was to hear her accuse her husband of it, and I wondered why she had. Was she being vindictive because he'd hurt her so many times by having affairs with other women? Or did she truly believe that Warren was capable of murder? One thing was certain: Nothing I said during our time together had convinced her otherwise.

The same driver who brought me to the house returned me to the Willard. I'd called George from the car, and we had arranged to meet for dinner at a favorite Washington spot of mine, the Foggy Bottom Café, a small, charming neighborhood restaurant in the River Inn, only a few blocks from the Kennedy Center.

The light was flashing on the telephone in my suite. I picked it up, pressed in the appropriate number for voice mail, and was told by a recorded voice that I had three messages.

The first was from a woman who identified herself as a reporter, Natalie Mumford. She said she wanted to speak with me concerning the death of Nikki Farlow, and left her number at the paper.

The second call was from George, who said he was tied up with some business and would be a half hour late meeting me at the restaurant.

The third was from Warren Nebel's press secretary, Sandy Teller, who announced it was urgent that he speak with me. He left the numbers for both his direct line at the senator's office and his cellular phone.

I returned the reporter's call and she picked up on the first ring. I could hear the sounds of a busy newsroom in the background.

"Thanks so much for getting back to me, Mrs. Fletcher," she said. "I'm working on the Nikki Farlow story and wondered if I could spend a few minutes with you."

"With me?" I said. "Why would you want to speak with me?"

"I understand you were the one who discovered the body."

"Quite by accident," I said. "I don't see why that would be of any interest to you as a reporter."

"Well, Mrs. Fletcher, I'm sure you can understand that when someone like Nikki Farlow is found murdered at the home of her boss, a United States senator, that's news here in Washington—or anywhere else, for that matter."

"Murder?"

"Yes. The police are now calling it a homicide."

"I wasn't aware of that."

"We just learned of it. Any chance of stealing fifteen minutes with you?"

"I suppose so, although this is shaping up to be a very busy week."

"I can be at your hotel in five minutes."

"Tonight? No, I'm afraid that's impossible. I'm about to leave to meet someone for dinner."

"How about fifteen minutes at the restaurant? Buy you and your friend a drink."

" I—"

"I promise no more than fifteen minutes. My watch has a timer."

I laughed. "All right," I said, "as long as you set that timer. But I must warn you, Ms. Mumford, I have nothing of interest to offer. I was simply a guest at the party along with many others."

"I realize that, Mrs. Fletcher, but you *were* there. I wasn't. I just want to get a sense of the mood at the house last night. You're a best-selling writer of murder mysteries. I'm sure your insight will be helpful. If you prefer, whatever you tell me will be on background. You have my word."

I'd learned over the years in dealing with the press that reporters often don't keep their word when they're after a story. They promise many things, but conveniently forget those promises when it serves their purpose. Her pledge to keep our conversation on background—not attributing anything I said to me by name—was comforting, provided she meant it, but I intended to stick to the facts and not offer any opinions. We agreed to meet at the Foggy Bottom Café, and she ended our conversation with, "I'm wearing a gray plaid skirt and blue blazer. Don't bother telling me what you're wearing, Mrs. Fletcher. I certainly know what you look like."

I next called the number Sandy Teller had left. He wasn't at the office, and I tried his cell phone.

"Good timing, Mrs. Fletcher," he said, sounding breathless. "I just got home. You've heard, I assume."

I knew what he was referring to but said, "Heard what?"

"That the police are now saying that Nikki was murdered, that it wasn't an accident."

"Yes, I did hear something about that."

"You'll be hearing a lot more, Mrs. Fletcher. I can guarantee you that. The press is already all over it. It'll be a media circus by tomorrow morning."

"I suppose that's inevitable," I said, "considering it happened at the home of a United States senator." I didn't add that the rumors of an affair between the senator and the victim would undoubtedly heighten press interest.

"How was your afternoon with Mrs. Nebel?"

"Lovely. We spent some pleasant time together."

"She's obviously upset about what happened."

"Understandably so."

"What did she have to say about it?"

I thought it a strange question for him to be asking me. What Pat Nebel and I spoke about was, and would continue to be, a private conversation between friends. My silence evidently wasn't lost on Teller, because he quickly said, "I don't mean to pry into what you and Mrs. Nebel said to each other. I suppose that . . . well . . . I suppose what I'm saying is that . . . well, let me put it this way, Mrs. Fletcher. The fact that you and your friend from England were the ones who discovered the body, and that you're a celebrity, will mean that the press will want to speak with you about Nikki's death. The senator is in the midst of a campaign for reelection, the worst possible timing for something like this to happen."

Even worse for Nikki Farlow, I thought.

"I'd like to suggest that we get together as soon as possible and coordinate how we handle the press."

"Coordinate?" I said. "I'm not sure I understand."

"I don't know how much experience you've had dealing with the press, Mrs. Fletcher, but I doubt you've seen them in a feeding frenzy. I've been doing this for years. It's my job as Senator Nebel's press secretary. The Washington press corps can be vicious, especially when a story involves a high-profile politician like the senator. It's my responsibility to see that he's protected from a media smear campaign. I'm sure you don't want to see that happen either."

I glanced at my watch, and realized I had to leave if I were to meet George on time. "Mr. Teller," I said, "I'm running late for a dinner appointment. I understand what your role is, but—"

"Has anyone from the press contacted you?" he asked bluntly.

I hesitated before replying, "Yes."

"Who?"

"A newspaper reporter."

"Who?"

"Mr. Teller, I appreciate your concern about Senator Nebel's political fortunes, but I don't think I have an obligation to keep you informed about who contacts me, and whom I choose to speak with."

"I thought you were a friend of the family."

"I am. At least, Pat Nebel and I are friends. I don't know the senator very well."

"All I'm asking for, Mrs. Fletcher, is a chance to meet

with you and outline what we're doing when it comes to dealing with the press on this matter. I'm not calling on my own. The senator asked me to contact you."

"All right. I'll meet with you," I said, anxious to get off the phone. "When?"

"Tomorrow morning? Eight?"

"Where?"

"I'll come to the hotel. Breakfast is on me."

"Very well; I'll see you then."

George was already at the Foggy Bottom Café when I walked in. Standing with him at the bar was a stunningly attractive woman wearing a gray plaid skirt and blue blazer.

"Ah, Jessica," he said, taking my hand and kissing me on the cheek. "This is—"

I smiled. "I know who this is," I said. "You must be Ms. Mumford."

She shook my hand and said, "Just my luck to end up meeting the person you're having dinner with. And someone from Scotland Yard as well."

"Drink, Jessica?" George asked. I saw that he'd already been served his favorite, a single-malt Scotch, and that the reporter had a glass of red wine.

"No, thanks," I said, thinking that I wanted to keep up my guard when talking to a reporter, and that an alcoholic beverage wouldn't help achieve that purpose. "But I am hungry. Shall we take a table?"

Once we were comfortably seated, George and I next to each other, Ms. Mumford across from us, I said, "I really would appreciate it if we could do this quickly. I haven't seen my friend here in a long time, and we have a lot of catching up to do."

A knowing smile played around her lips and she said, winking at me, "If I were meeting such a handsome inspector from Scotland Yard, I'd want to find as much time alone with him as possible, too."

I ignored the comment and said, "You told me on the phone that the police now consider the death at Senator Nebel's house last night to be murder. From whom did you hear that?"

"The detective in charge of the case," Mumford said.

"Detective Moody?"

"Yes. He's the one who told me you'd discovered the body."

"Not me alone," I said. "George and I were together."

"Of course. Look, I'll level with you, Mrs. Fletcher. I don't know if you're aware that rumors have been circulating around this city that Senator Nebel was carrying on a long-term affair with the deceased."

I said nothing, not wanting to confirm or deny what she'd said.

She continued: "When a member of Congress is accused of having an affair with someone who works for him, and that someone ends up missing—remember Gary Condit?—or is found dead at the foot of a set of stairs at that elected official's house, what was once just an indiscretion becomes a big story. You were at that dinner party, Mrs. Fletcher. I wasn't. What I'm trying to do is get your impressions of the people who were there, and what you think might have happened to Nikki Farlow. You not only have a reputation as a wonderful writer of murder mysteries, but you seem to have ended up in the middle of real-life murders more than once. So tell me, what's your take on what happened last night?"

George said, "I'm sure you're aware, Miss Mumford, that having someone of Mrs. Fletcher's stature helping you with your story adds a certain—how shall I say it?—panache?"

"Sure it does," she agreed. She looked at me. "Do you think Farlow was murdered?"

I looked at George before answering. "What I think doesn't really matter, Ms. Mumford. If it was a murder, it's strictly a police matter."

"True," she said, "but someone who was there last night tells me that Detective Moody spent quite a bit of time with you and Inspector Sutherland. Why was that?"

George answered: "Because we were the ones who discovered the body."

"I also understand that Mrs. Nebel wasn't there," Mumford said.

"She wasn't feeling well," I said.

"Strange, isn't it, that his wife, who's heading up this Literacy Week, wouldn't be at a dinner party celebrating it?"

"Not at all," I said, looking at my watch. "I think we've spent our fifteen minutes together, Ms. Mumford. To be honest with you, I really have nothing to offer. A woman died an unfortunate death last night, and Inspector Sutherland and I happened to be there. Mrs. Nebel is an old friend of mine from back home in Cabot Cove, and I don't think it's appropriate for me to be discussing personal things about her family, particularly allegations of an affair between her husband and the victim. I wish I had more to offer but I simply don't."

She sat back, smiled, and nodded. "I get the hint," she said. "And I really appreciate the opportunity to talk to you like this. Mind if I keep in touch?"

"No, of course not."

She'd been taking notes. She folded her long, slim reporter's notebook, capped her pen, and stood. Then, as a practiced afterthought, she asked, "Any talk at the party about congressional funny money?"

George and I stared at her blankly.

"Thanks again," she said. "We'll be in touch. Oh, by the way, don't be surprised if people in this town start speculating that Senator Nebel might have been the one who killed his paramour. If nothing else, his political enemies will make sure that possibility is floated."

"How unfortunate," I said.

She shrugged. "Welcome to Washington, D.C."

Chapter Eight

Once Natalie Mumford left the restaurant, George and I deliberately avoided discussing the events of the previous night.

He'd certainly been busy since the last time I'd seen him. He'd been appointed by the Yard as its coordinator on terrorism, necessitating his meeting with others involved in antiterrorism activities from around the world. Like every other thinking, concerned citizen, I'd given a lot of thought, and had been concerned about, the wanton destruction terrorists had heaped upon the world, especially in New York City and Washington, and what the future might hold. But I knew only what I'd read in papers and magazines, or seen on television. George's inside knowledge of the world's war on terrorism went far beyond what's been recounted in the popular press, and I hung on every word.

By the time we stepped outside the restaurant on to

25th Street NW, the unsettled weather had given way to a cloudless, starlit sky, and we decided to take a postprandial walk to the Kennedy Center, where a show had just let out and people came streaming from one of many theaters in the complex. We entered the building, named after the slain president, and took the elevator to the terrace, built over a highway, from which the view of the river and Georgetown beyond was spectacular.

"It's a lovely city," George said as we stood at a railing and took in the sights.

"I've always liked Washington," I said. "The buildings are beautiful, especially at night. It's a Southern city really, more slow-paced than New York or Chicago."

"But not as slow-paced as your Cabot Cove," he said, chuckling and lighting his pipe.

"That's right," I said. "I love the hustle-bustle of big cities, but always enjoy getting back home to my small town. Of course, Cabot Cove is growing, too, people from big cities looking for a more peaceful way of life."

"What did you think of Ms. Mumford?" he asked.

"What did *you* think of her?" I asked.

"Attractive woman."

"I noticed you noticed," I said playfully.

"Was my appreciation that obvious? I thought she was pleasant enough. Journalists can be so bloody meddlesome, but I appreciate the job they have to do."

"I feel the same way. But I felt I didn't need to inform her of everything I know. Pat Nebel says she thinks her husband might have killed Nikki Farlow."

My offhand comment caused him to cough. He removed the pipe from his mouth and said, "That's startling. Usually a wife stands behind her man."

"In most cases, yes. She claims to have overheard a conversation between her husband and his lawyer that indicated, at least to her, that Nikki was blackmailing Warren over an affair they'd been having."

"Leave it to you, Jessica, to come up with information like that. I assume the police aren't aware of Mrs. Nebel's suspicions."

"I hope not, at least for the senator's sake. He's received death threats, you know."

"No, I didn't know. Will you share what Mrs. Nebel told you with the police?"

"I suppose I should."

"Death threats, you say? Since last night?"

I shook my head. "No, no. A while ago. I read it in our local paper before I left home. They have to do with his vote on locating the nuclear power plant near Cabot Cove."

He resumed puffing on his pipe and looked out over the river. A brisk, welcome breeze came up and ruffled my hair. It felt good.

"I wonder if Ms. Farlow's death—murder, it now seems to be—had anything to do with that power plant and the senator's stand on it," he mused.

"I hadn't considered that, although I don't see the connection."

"What is the senator's stand on that issue?"

"Ironically, he seems to represent the sole undecided vote. At least that's how I understand it. It's hard to fathom, not only for me, but for a lot of my neighbors, too. I remember when he was running for his second term. The issue was floating around even then, and he made speeches against locating the plant there. 'It will be built here over my dead body,' is what he said. But he's made speeches since in which he's pointed to the jobs the plant would create, and the boost to the Cabot Cove economy in general. I suppose I understand his conflict, and I wouldn't want to be in his shoes, having to make such a decision."

"That's a powerful position to be in."

"What is?"

"Holding the crucial vote. I imagine he's on the receiving end of considerable persuasion."

I thought back to the conversation we'd had at the dinner party with Joe Radisch, Christine Nebel's fiancé. He'd made a snide comment about the senator's lavish lifestyle, insinuating that Nebel might be the recipient of illegal contributions. And the reporter, Ms. Mumford, had asked about "funny money."

"Do you know what Ms. Farlow's position was on the power plant, Jessica?"

"No, I don't, although I have to assume it mirrored the senator's view. It would be awkward if his top aide didn't agree with his views."

"Quite so," George said. "Feel like a nightcap?"

"If it will extend the evening," I said, taking his arm as we headed for the elevator.

A turbaned cabdriver drove us to the Willard, where we'd decided to end our night together. We walked into the Round Robin Bar off the lobby, a handsome room with a green hunt-club décor and a huge, circular mahogany bar manned by two bartenders in starched white jackets and black bow ties. We found a table for two in a secluded corner; the other tables were occupied by prosperous-looking men and women, adding credence to the hotel's reputation for attracting Washington's movers and shakers.

"What's on your agenda tomorrow?" he asked once we'd been served.

"I'm not certain. The schedule for the literacy program has me on the run. But now that I've agreed to spend time with Pat Nebel, I'm not sure what that will do to the schedule. You?"

"Relatively free. Up for breakfast?"

"Already committed. I'm having breakfast here at the hotel as a matter of fact, with Senator Nebel's press secretary, Sandy Teller."

"About the literacy program?"

"No. He wants to talk to me about what happened last night at the house, and what ramifications it could have for the senator. He also wants to give me tips for handling the press."

"Strange."

"What's strange?"

"That he wants to speak to *you* about that."

"I thought the same thing, and tried to dissuade him. But Senator Nebel evidently asked that we meet. At least that's what Mr. Teller said."

"I don't doubt that the senator did," George said. He

paused before adding, "Do you get the feeling, Jessica, that the senator and his people might be using you?"

"The thought has recently crossed my mind—as recently as a few minutes ago—but I prefer not to believe it."

"Which I can understand. I know you don't need my advice, but I'll offer it anyway."

"Your advice is always welcome, George."

"Distance yourself from the senator and Ms. Farlow's murder. Devote yourself to the reason you're here in Washington, your friend's literacy program. Let the police worry about Ms. Farlow's murder, and any ramifications it might have for Senator Nebel."

His were words of wisdom, and caused me to fall silent. George sensed the internal debate I was going through, placed his hand on my arm, and said, "But I also know you, Jessica Fletcher. You're loyal to your friend, Mrs. Nebel, which is an admirable trait. *And* you have this penchant for seeing that justice is done."

I turned to him. "You're right, of course," I said. "I do feel a responsibility to Patricia Nebel. *And*, as you so eloquently point out, I do have a penchant for seeing justice done. Not to mention that when I find myself involved in a murder case—which I might add has happened on occasion through no fault or deliberate action on my part— I'm naturally inclined to follow up on it." I shrugged and raised my hands in a gesture of resignation. "That's me, George, for better or for worse."

"All part of your charm, Jessica. But I might point out that this particular murder has happened in your nation's capital, at the home of one of your highest elected officials, and seems to be wrapped up in an affair between that elected official and the deceased. A heady scenario, I'm sure you'll agree. Just be careful, my dear."

I sat back and looked around the room. The other customers in the Willard exuded the sort of power for which Washington, D.C., is famous, and I knew George was right in how he'd characterized the situation surrounding Nikki Farlow's death. As I was pondering his words, Walter Grusin, the lobbyist for Sterling Power, the nuclear power company, entered the bar with two other people, a man, and a woman I recognized as the congresswoman from California, Gail Marshall-Miner. I turned my back to the door, but not in time to avoid being spotted by him. He waved; after he and the others had been seated, he came to our table.

"Good evening Mrs. Fletcher," he said through a broad smile. "Inspector."

"Good evening," we replied.

"Enjoying yourself?"

"Very much."

"Care to join us?"

"Thank you, no."

"I'm still hoping to get some time with you," he said.

"Well," I said, "the week seems to be getting busier every hour."

He glanced back at his table, where drink orders were being taken, leaned closer to me, and said, "If you meet with me and allow me to make my case, Mrs. Fletcher, you might find it to your benefit."

"Maybe I would," I said, ignoring the insinuation that

there might be a *tangible* benefit to me. "Yes, as a matter of fact, I'd like to hear what you have to say about locating the plant near Cabot Cove. I'll call you when I'm free."

"Wonderful," he said, laying his business card on the table. "I'll look forward to hearing from you." He bade us a good night and returned to his guests.

"I must say you're a constant source of surprises," George said. "I never thought you'd indulge him like that."

"Sometimes I surprise myself," I said. "But now that I've decided to see what I can do to get to the bottom of Nikki Farlow's murder, I'll need to talk to as many people who were at the party as possible."

"As many *suspects* as possible," he said.

"Exactly."

"I hate to judge people based upon so little contact, but I must admit I don't particularly like Mr. Grusin, the lobbyist," George said, motioning for our check.

I watched Grusin laughing loudly at something Congresswoman Marshall-Miner had said, and started laughing myself.

"What's funny?" George asked, placing his credit card on the bill.

"I read that Ulysses S. Grant coined the term *lobbyist* here at the Willard because of the people hanging around the lobby hoping to corner influential politicians. I wonder if he had someone like Mr. Grusin in mind."

"Perhaps he did. After all, Grusin came over here to corner an influential person named J. B. Fletcher."

"Well," I said, "he succeeded, didn't he? This was a

lovely evening, George. I'm glad we had a chance to spend some time together."

"Let's not make it the last time. I'm at liberty, and at your beck and call." He wrote something on the back of his business card and handed it to me. "My cell number. Call me whenever you have a free moment and I'll be there."

We regretfully parted in Peacock Alley, the block-long, palm-lined promenade in the heart of the hotel's grand and harmonious lobby, where famous clientele of old had strutted their stuff. When he wasn't writing in his suite, Mark Twain was reported to have strolled its length each day, resplendent in his signature white linen suit with matching hair and mustache, and then to have done it again in case anyone missed him the first time.

"Sleep tight, Mrs. Fletcher. And remember that you don't have to single-handedly solve the murder of Miss Nikki Farlow."

"And you remember that although you're a big, strong Scotland Yard inspector, it doesn't make you immortal. The crime rate in Washington, I'm told, is far above the national average."

"Jessica, I—"

"Just don't let anything happen to you, George. Good night."

He leaned down and kissed me gently on the lips. "Good night."

I stood for a moment, watching him leave the hotel. He turned just before the door and smiled.

I smiled back.

Chapter Nine

Sandy Teller called me the next morning from a house phone.

"Good morning, Mrs. Fletcher."

"Good morning. Are you here in the hotel?"

"Yes."

"I'll be down in a few minutes."

He was waiting at the entrance to the hotel's Willard Room restaurant. We shook hands and went to where a maître d' stood ready to seat people.

"Good morning, Mr. Teller," the maître d' said. "How nice to see you again."

"Thank you," Teller replied, his attention not on the maître d' but on the room itself, which was already partially filled with customers.

"I have a nice table by the window for you," the maître d' said.

Teller turned to me. "Mind a change in plans, Mrs. Fletcher?"

"Meaning?" I asked.

"We'll have breakfast someplace else. Too many media types in there this morning."

Without explaining anything to the maître d', he took my elbow, guided me across the lobby to the front entrance, and hailed a taxi that waited in line with other cabs.

"Sorry for the sudden change," he said, "but I don't need a bunch of reporters asking questions off the record." He told the driver to take us to the Dirksen Senate office building. "We'll have something there. Hope that's okay with you."

"I suppose it will have to be," I said, finding it strange that we couldn't have breakfast in a public place. But since my only other option was to insist the cabdriver stop and let me off, I acquiesced.

After being checked through security, including a metal detector, we went to Senator Nebel's office suite, where his staff was already busy at work despite the early hour. I spotted Nikki Farlow's assistant, Richard Carraway, in a cubicle at the far end of the large outer office. He wiggled his fingers at me in a gesture of welcome, which I returned.

"Grab a seat here," Teller said, indicating a table with two vacant chairs. "I'll order up breakfast. Continental okay with you?"

"That will be fine," I said. "Please make it tea instead of coffee. And tomato juice."

"Sure thing," he said, disappearing into what I assumed was his own office and shutting the door behind him.

After ten minutes had passed, I became annoyed at the circumstances I'd found myself in, and was about to get up to leave when Carraway came from his cubicle and joined me at the table.

"How are you holding up, Mrs. Fletcher?" he asked.

"Holding up? I'm 'holding up' quite nicely, thank you, although I don't know the reason why I'm sitting here this morning." I gathered up my handbag. "Perhaps you'd be good enough to tell Mr. Teller that I've left."

I'd no sooner said that when the door to Teller's office opened and he motioned for me. For a moment I considered ignoring him and simply walking out of the office. But my curiosity demanded an explanation of his behavior, and I followed him into his office, a cluttered space with every inch of his desk covered with mounds of paper, newspapers, and magazines.

"Sorry, Mrs. Fletcher," he said, removing a pile of materials from a chair and inviting me to sit. "I thought I'd better get in here and handle the most pressing media calls before sitting down with you."

A young woman opened the door and delivered breakfast.

"Ah, nourishment has arrived," Teller said, moving another pile of papers on the front of his desk to accommodate the tray. He took an empty cup and a carafe of coffee and resumed his seat behind the desk.

I didn't have much of an appetite, but dutifully broke off a piece of croissant and took a sip of tomato juice.

Teller held up a sheaf of pink message slips. "See these?" he said. "All calls from the media about what happened to Nikki, and this is just the beginning. They're vultures, reporters, and they won't stop until they get the story *they* want, whether it represents the truth or not."

"I hope I never become that cynical," I said. "I've always considered the press to be the real check and balance on our government, although I am well aware of their excesses."

"I wish I could share your sanguine view of the media," he said, tossing the message slips on the desk like a poker player throwing in his hand. "Have you spoken with Mrs. Nebel this morning?"

"No, I haven't. But let me ask you something, Mr. Teller. I agreed to have breakfast with you this morning primarily because you said Senator Nebel had asked for us to meet. Instead of having breakfast at the hotel, as planned, you whisked me away in a taxi and sat me down at a table while you went off to do whatever it is you do for the senator. Frankly, I have no idea why I'm here."

Teller, deeply tanned and with pale blue eyes, nodded in agreement. Or wanted me to think he agreed. He said, "Let me level with you, Mrs. Fletcher."

"I wish you would."

"As you know, the senator is in a tight race for another term in the Senate. He's being attacked from all sides over a variety of issues. That's bad enough. But now his top aide is found dead at his home after a dinner party, and the rumormongers here in Washington are dredging up baseless allegations that he and Nikki had been getting it on. Having an affair. An office romance. Do you know what that can do to his reelection chances?"

"Obviously it won't help. But that doesn't answer my question, Mr. Teller. What does it have to do with me?"

"It has to do with you, Mrs. Fletcher, because you're a friend of the senator's wife—and that means you've probably been privy to things she's been saying about the rumors concerning the senator and Nikki."

"Even if I had been, I certainly wouldn't share them with anyone else."

"Yeah, I'm sure you wouldn't, except that the press can be pretty good at getting people to say things they don't want to say. You said you'd been contacted by somebody from the *Post*. Natalie Mumford?"

"Yes, as a matter of fact."

"What did you tell her?"

"That, Mr. Teller, is none of your business."

He laughed. "You're right, but I'll find out anyway when I read what she writes. And if you've messed up," he said, "I'm the one who will have to clean up after you." He swiveled in his chair and looked out a small window, then returned his attention to me. "Because you're Pat Nebel's friend, Mrs. Fletcher, I'm sure you're aware that she's not the most—how can I put this gently?—she's not the most stable of people."

"Stable?" I said, unable to keep the anger out of my voice.

"Don't get me wrong," he said defensively. "Pat is a terrific person, and I personally am very fond of her."

How nice, I thought.

"But she's never tried to hide the fact that she dislikes politics, considers it a dirty business. That's posed a lot of problems for the senator over the years he's been in Washington. What he needs most at a time like this is the unflinching backing of his wife, someone to stand at his side and dismiss these rumors about an affair with Nikki for what they are, nothing but malicious gossip by his enemies."

"I'm sure she does stand by him," I said, not entirely meaning it, based upon the conversation I'd had with her the previous day.

"You mark my words, Mrs. Fletcher; it's only a matter of time before the senator is accused of killing Nikki because of their alleged affair. It doesn't matter that it's a lie. Once a rumor starts spreading in Washington, it develops legs. It becomes the truth even when it isn't." He pointed at the empty china cup in front of me. "You haven't had your tea," he said.

"I'm not in the mood, and I really think I ought to be going. I'm here in Washington for the literacy program and would like to catch up with the others."

Teller stood, came around the desk, and leaned back against it. "I'm trying to convince the senator to issue a public statement about Nikki's death, take the offense and head things off at the pass. I'm hoping he'll go along with it, and I want Mrs. Nebel right there at his side. I'd like you there, too."

I, too, stood. "I don't think that would be appropriate," I said.

The door opened and Nebel stuck his head in.

"Jessica, how wonderful to see you. I knew you and

Sandy were breaking bread together this morning, but didn't know it would be here at the office." To Teller: "The least you could do for our distinguished guest from Cabot Cove is to take her to a decent restaurant, Sandy."

"Breakfast was fine," I said, "but I'm just leaving."

"Give me a few minutes before you go?" Nebel asked.

I sighed and nodded.

In his private office, he struck a pose at the window and looked out over Washington, saying without looking at me, "These are challenging days for our country. So much is at stake here and abroad, and it's going to take clear thinking and a commitment to our democratic ideals to see us move forward."

He turned and said to me, "I understand you're against the power plant in Cabot Cove."

"I don't know where you got that information, Senator, but I do have serious reservations about it."

"That vote is coming up soon in the Senate, and it represents perhaps one of the most important votes I'll ever cast in that body. I have an obligation to my constituents in Maine, and the polls tell me the majority of them are against the plant. On the other hand, as a senator, I am also expected to make decisions that will benefit the greatest number of people—despite the polls. That plant could prevent another serious blackout up and down the East Coast, to say nothing of providing jobs in our state and pumping money into the economy. You're one of the most well-known people in Maine, Jessica. Hell, in the world, for that matter. It's important that I have your support no matter which direction I go."

"I'm sorry, Senator, but I don't involve myself in politics. I'm sure you'll do whatever you feel is best."

And suffer the consequences at the ballot box, I thought.

He instantly changed the subject. "Pat said you had a nice talk," he said. "I really appreciate your spending time with her this week."

"It was my pleasure."

"Pat is going to need you more than ever, Jessica."

I started to say something, but he continued.

"My political opponents will use Nikki's tragic death to smear me, to claim she and I were having an affair. Hell, I won't be surprised if they start accusing me of having killed her. You've heard that the police are now considering it a murder?"

"Yes."

"I think they're on the wrong track, but I don't have any control over that." His laugh was grim. "You'd think as a senator you'd have all sorts of power, could control the destiny of everything. But that isn't true. Look, all I can ask is that you continue to stand by Pat's side in this difficult time."

And by extension be at your side, too.

He picked up the phone and told someone to arrange for a car to pick me up in front of the building.

"That's not necessary," I said.

He ignored me, picked up the phone again, and said, "Richard, there's a car coming for Mrs. Fletcher downstairs. Please escort her there."

"No, no need for that," I said. "I can find my way out."

"Nonsense. I insist."

I lingered another few minutes in his office until he was informed that the car had arrived. We shook hands. As he was about to open the door for me, a female scream erupted from the other side of it.

"What the hell?" he said.

"Get down!" a male voice yelled. The sound of people scurrying about could be heard.

"What are you, some sort of a madman?" someone yelled. "Put down that damn gun!"

Gun?

Nebel's face was ashen. We both took a few steps back, away from the door, just before it was thrown open by Richard Carraway, his face a mask of fear and confusion. Behind him stood an older man pointing a handgun at us.

Nebel left my side and sought refuge behind his tall desk chair, leaving me staring into the face of the gun-wielding man. Carraway, who'd come through the door, ducked behind it, leaving the man and me to lock eyes.

"Oscar?" I said.

"Mrs. Fletcher?"

Like every town in America, Cabot Cove has its resident eccentrics, and Oscar Brophy was one of them. He lived by himself on the outskirts of Cabot Cove and was known as a loner, a man with a temper, although I'd never heard of him actually hurting anyone. Despite a rough-hewn appearance and way of speaking, he was a voracious reader, spending his days at the local library, where he checked out dozens of books each week, most of them on history and current events. I'd often bumped into him there, and he regularly attended talks I'd given at the library, always the first person to arrive to secure a seat in the front row. He'd worked at a mill, had been injured on the job, and now lived on disability payments and his monthly Social Security check.

"What are you doing with that gun, Oscar? I suggest you put it down *now!*"

His eyes darted left and right and his lips trembled. Still, he held the gun in both hands, aimed directly at me.

"He ain't going to build no nuke plant next to my house," he said, his quavering voice mirroring the flustered expression on his craggy face. He wore a frayed brown corduroy jacket over a plaid flannel shirt and overalls. "These damn politicians don't care anything about us regular people, sell their mother to get elected."

"That may be true, Oscar," I said, trying to keep my voice steady, "but coming here like this with a gun and threatening people is not the answer. Please put down that gun. I promise I'll try to help you, but only if you do what I say."

For a moment I thought he was going to pull the trigger, maybe not deliberately, but because of a tremor causing both arms to shake. Then, to my profound relief, he lowered the weapon. As he did, two of Nebel's young male staff members jumped on him, wrestling him to the floor and pinning his arms behind him.

"Don't hurt him," I said, approaching. Someone in the outer office had called security, and a half dozen uniformed Capitol Hill policemen came bursting through the door, guns drawn.

"You know him?" Carraway said to me after the police

had gotten Oscar to his feet and placed handcuffs on his wrists and shackles on his ankles.

"Yes, I know him," I said. I thought back to the newspaper article claiming that Senator Nebel had received death threats, and wondered whether they'd come from Oscar.

The senator came out from behind his desk and joined me in the outer office.

"How the hell did he get through security?" he demanded.

Sandy Teller, who'd stayed in his office with the door closed during the fracas, now entered the outer office and said, "I'll get to the bottom of it." He ran from the office, followed by Carraway and the two male assistants who'd tackled Oscar.

"My God," Nebel said to me. "We might have been killed."

I'd taken a chair because my legs were shaky. I looked up at him and said, "I think you'd better worry about how someone carrying a gun got through that metal detector downstairs." I stood, brushed off my skirt, and said, "In the meantime, that car is waiting for me, and I intend to take it."

I rode an elevator down to the lobby and approached security from the inside of the building, where Teller, Carraway, and the others were in an animated conversation with the security guards. By this time, a SWAT team from the Capitol Police had descended on the building and taken up positions in the lobby and out on the sidewalk.

Teller saw me heading for the door and stopped me.

"Looks like you were in the wrong place at the wrong time again, Mrs. Fletcher."

"I'm afraid you're right," I said, "and hopefully it will be the last time while I'm in Washington."

I stepped outside and went to where an older gentleman in a black chauffeur's uniform stood next to the open passenger door of a Lincoln Town Car.

"I'm Jessica Fletcher," I said. "Are you here for me?"

"Yes, ma'am."

The driver closed the door behind me, got behind the wheel, and we pulled away from the Dirksen Building. He asked over his shoulder, "What's going on there? Somebody was yelling that a guy with a gun was trying to kill a senator."

"So I heard," I said, "but I'm sure everything turned out all right. The Library of Congress, please."

Chapter Ten

When I arrived at the Madison Building, a discussion group had just commenced, led by the Library of Congress's head of the rare books section. I apologized for being late and slipped into a chair at a far end of the table. It was a spirited discussion about ways to encourage young people to read more, suggestions running the gamut from mounting a television ad campaign on shows popular with youth, to paying students for each book they read. I tried to focus on the conversation, but kept thinking back to Oscar Brophy and his woefully misguided attempt to influence Senator Nebel's vote on the nuclear power plant.

I was pleased to see that Patricia Nebel was there, although I had the feeling she would have preferred not to be. She looked as though she hadn't had much sleep the night before, her expression vacant and distracted, wrapped in sadness. She barely acknowledged my arrival, and I wondered what her night had been like, whether she'd had discussions with her husband about Nikki Farlow's death, now termed a homicide, and about the allegations that he and his aide had been involved in a sexual relationship.

I'd been there a half hour when Eleanor Atherton, the library's public affairs representative, interrupted the meeting and asked if she could speak with me. I followed her into the hallway.

"I just heard about what happened this morning at Senator Nebel's office," she said. "What a fright it must have been."

"It was upsetting," I said.

"They say you knew the man who attempted to kill the senator."

"Oh," I said, "I really doubt if Oscar would have shot him. I—"

"They say you talked him out of it," she said.

"Who is 'they'?" I asked.

"The media. Reporters have tracked you down here and are clamoring to speak with you. The phone is ringing off the hook in my office."

"Oh, my," I said, thinking of Sandy Teller's comment that I'd ended up in the wrong place at the wrong time—again. I certainly wasn't in a position to argue with him.

"Would you like to come to my office, Jessica?" Ms. Atherton said. "To return calls?"

"I'm not sure I want to return calls from reporters, but I would like some time to gather my thoughts."

"Of course."

I declined an offer of tea or coffee as she led me into a small room off her office that appeared to be a multiuse space. Floor-to-ceiling steel shelving held boxes of paper, envelopes, and other office supplies. A TV set was tuned to one of the cable news channels; two young women sorted papers on a round table in one corner.

"We use this room to gather and file press clippings about the library," Atherton explained. "These are two of our interns from GW's journalism school."

After I'd been introduced to them, Atherton politely asked them to leave, and closed the door behind them. She, too, left me alone for a few minutes before returning with a handful of phone messages she'd collected for me.

"All these?" I said, hearing a constantly ringing phone on the other side of the closed door.

"Afraid so."

"I'm sorry to be putting you to all this trouble," I said.

"Don't worry about that, Jessica. Happy to help in any way we can."

I pulled my cell phone from my purse. "I left it off this morning," I said as I powered it up and saw a small icon on the screen indicating that messages had been stored in its memory. I pushed a few more buttons on the keypad and listened as a recorded female voice told me who had called. "You have three new messages," she said through the speaker. They were from George Sutherland, Seth Hazlitt in Cabot Cove, and Detective Joe Moody.

"Jessica," George said, "I'm in my hotel room watching the telly and the news came on about your being in Senator Nebel's office when some madman with a gun tried to kill him. They say he's a friend of yours. Are you all right? Please call as soon as you receive this."

Seth said, "Been watchin' television, Jessica, and heard about Oscar Brophy pullin' some dumb stunt in Senator Nebel's office. Damn fool. Glad nobody got killed, including you. The fella on TV said you were the one who talked Oscar into givin' up his gun. Sounds like we'd have a dead senator if you weren't there. Give me a call, heah?"

Detective Moody's call didn't have anything to do with the scene in Nebel's Capitol Hill office: "Mrs. Fletcher, this is Joe Moody, Fairfax police. I'd appreciate a chance to speak with you at your earliest convenience. It has to do with the Farlow case. Thank you." He left his number.

"I'd better return these," I said.

"Sure," Atherton said. "I'll leave you alone."

Seth wanted to know everything that had happened in Nebel's office that morning, and I gave him a quick rundown, ending with, "Poor Oscar. He's— Oh, wait. There's something on TV."

I'd not seen any TV reports about the incident, and listened and watched intently as a female anchor recounted what had happened. It was reported as an attempted murder of a United States senator, and that Capitol police had turned Brophy over to local authorities. The closing words made me wince: "Noted mystery writer Jessica Fletcher, who's reported to be a friend of the accused, is said by others in Nebel's office to have talked the assailant into surrendering his weapon. Mrs. Fletcher, here in Washington from her home in Maine as part of a literacy initiative mounted by Senator Nebel and his wife,

Patricia, was also present when the senator's aide, Nikki Farlow, was found murdered following a dinner party at Nebel's home two nights ago, and was the one who discovered the body along with another guest, a Scotland Yard inspector."

"What are they sayin'?" Seth asked.

"Nothing that I haven't told you already."

"Well, all I can say is that you take care while you're down there in Washington. Got the highest murder rate per capita in the whole darn country."

"I will," I said. He obviously hadn't heard yet about Nikki Farlow's murder.

George answered on the first ring. "Where are you?" he immediately asked.

"At the Library of Congress. I was in a meeting when—"

"I'll be there in ten minutes, fifteen at the most."

"George, I—"

"No argument, Jessica. You need a—what do your politicians call it?—you need a handler to keep you out of trouble."

"Oh, George, that's—"

"Will you be in front?"

I sighed. "Yes, I'll be in front."

I went into Ms. Atherton's office and told her I was leaving.

"What shall I tell the others from your group?" she asked.

"Tell them I was called away unexpectedly, but that I'll catch up with them later."

She walked me to the building entrance. "Sure you're all right?" she asked.

"Yes, I'm fine."

"Sometimes the shock of what you've been through takes a while to hit home."

I smiled to reassure her. "Don't worry about me," I said. "Thanks for all your courtesies."

I waited inside the main entrance until I saw a taxi pull up, and George jumped out. I left the building to meet him and was immediately accosted by a reporter holding a microphone tethered to a video camera on a colleague's shoulder.

"Mrs. Fletcher, Jean Watson from Fox News. Tell us what happened this morning at Senator Nebel's office."

"Please," I said, "I have nothing to say."

George came to my side.

"Are you the Scotland Yard inspector who discovered Nikki Farlow's body with Mrs. Fletcher?" he was asked.

George maintained his silence as he led me to the waiting cab. Once settled inside, he told the driver to take us to his hotel, the Westin, where we went into the hotel's café fronting M Street. An iced tea in front of me, iced coffee in front of him, he said, "Tell me about what happened to you this morning."

I filled him in between sips.

"Looks like you're on your way to becoming the most famous person in Washington," he said.

"Hardly what I aspired to when I came here," I said. "That reporter knew who you were, too."

"How did you end up at the senator's office?"

"Senator Nebel's press secretary decided to not have breakfast at the hotel and took me to the office. I was about to leave when Oscar arrived."

"The man must be demented."

"He's eccentric," I said. "But I don't think he would have actually harmed anyone."

"An eccentric in a great deal of trouble."

"Unfortunately true. I got a call from Detective Moody this morning on my cell phone."

"What does he want?"

"He left a message saying it's about Ms. Farlow's murder."

"No surprise. What other reason would he have to call you?"

"None. I haven't returned the call yet. Maybe I should do it now."

Detective Moody was summoned to the phone by the officer who answered, and thanked me for getting back to him. "I see you've had an interesting morning, Mrs. Fletcher," he said.

"One I'd rather forget," I said.

"I'd like to speak with you . Any chance of meeting me at Senator Nebel's house this afternoon?"

"At the house?"

"Yes. There are some things I'd like to go over with you there."

"I suppose that would be all right. Have you informed the Nebels?"

"No, but I will. Can you be there at two?"

"Yes. I'll be with Inspector Sutherland."

Silence on his end either indicated that he'd lost his train of thought, or wasn't pleased to hear about George.

"That'll be fine. Two o'clock."

"I take it we're to meet with the detective," George said after I'd clicked off the phone.

"I hope you don't mind my committing you."

"Not at all." He smiled.

"You're amused at something," I said.

"I'm smiling, Jessica, because I sense you're about to go to work."

"Go to work?"

"Put on your sleuth's hat and solve the murder of one Nikki Farlow."

"Do you disapprove?"

"Not in the least, as long as you allow me to partner with you. My conference has wrapped up and I've put in for a week's leave, so I have nothing but time on my hands. I don't play golf, find most films these days to be sophomoric bores, and am not much of a tourist. Besides, the thought of you being left to your own devices here in Washington sends a chill up my spine."

"Are you suggesting I'm not capable of solving a murder on my own?"

"Absolutely not. But we've paired up before in such situations and done quite nicely, you might remember."

"Napa, California," I said, not able to suppress a smile at remembering being together in that beautiful wine country when a former Hollywood director turned vintner was murdered.

"Scotland," he said.

"Ah, yes, Scotland," I said, recalling having visited George's family castle in Wick, Scotland, with a contingent of friends from Cabot Cove and ending up smack-dab in the middle of a murder there.

"And London," he offered, referring to when we'd first met. I'd become a suspect in the murder of a dear friend, and George had investigated the crime.

"We're meeting Detective Moody at two, at the Nebel house."

"Returning to the scene of the crime."

"Something like that."

"What about your obligations to the literacy drive? That's what brought you here in the first place."

"I'll take part in what I can. Ready?"

"Where are we going?" he asked as we left the café.

"To Senator Nebel's office."

"Might I ask why?"

"I can't think of a better place to start. As unpleasant a thought as it might be, Nikki Farlow was killed at the senator's home, by someone he'd invited to his dinner party. Whether the motive was personal, professional, or political, that *someone* is linked to the—to *my* junior senator from Maine."

Chapter Eleven

Security at the Dirksen Building had been beefed up considerably compared to earlier that morning. There were twice as many security guards on duty, and bags and briefcases were thoroughly searched. We eventually passed inspection and rode the elevator to the floor on which Warren Nebel's suite was located.

The office was a beehive of activity when we entered. I saw through the open door to Sandy Teller's office that he had two phones in his hands, one pressed to each ear. Richard Carraway was hunched over a computer, his eyes focused on the screen. A half dozen young staffers seemed to be in perpetual motion in the large outer office, answering phones, working at computers, their expressions promising that the fate of the free world rested with them.

The senator's personal secretary, who manned a desk just outside his private office, greeted me. "Good morning Mrs. Fletcher," she said. "Back so soon?"

"Good morning," I said. "This is Inspector George Sutherland, of Scotland Yard."

"Good morning to you, sir."

"Is the senator available?" I asked.

She nodded toward the closed door. "He's in there with investigators from the Capitol Police, and detectives from the Metropolitan Police Department."

"Do you expect he'll be with them long?" I asked.

"Hard to say. I'll let him know you're here."

She buzzed his office and announced we were waiting to see him. She hung up the phone and said, "He said he didn't think he'd be much longer. Have a seat."

George and I sat in orange plastic chairs near her desk and continued to take in the activity around us. George seemed especially interested in Carraway, probably because I'd told him during the cab ride that the Senate aide gave me the impression during dinner that he was not particularly fond of his boss, Nikki Farlow. Not that that meant he'd murdered her. Lots of people dislike their bosses but don't go to the extent of killing them. Still, when someone has been murdered, certain groups of people become prime suspects, beginning with spouses or lovers, followed closely by those who've expressed or were known to have a particular dislike for the victim.

Based upon my brief encounter with people at the dinner party, I'd tried to come up with my own shortlist of those who might have had a motive to kill Nikki. Besides Carraway, there was the senator himself. If he'd been having an affair with her—and was being blackmailed to keep the affair quiet—his anger, coupled with the threat she posed to his reelection bid, might be sufficient to have prompted him to take drastic action.

Too, as much as I hated to admit it, the hurt that Nebel's alleged affair had inflicted upon his wife, Patricia, could well have brought her to the brink of wanting to see Nikki dead.

Of course, anyone present at the Nebel house the night Nikki died had to be considered a suspect, unless she'd been killed by someone with no apparent connection to the senator and his guests. I doubted that was the case. The dock was virtually unreachable unless you used the long set of wooden stairs leading from the house, and I hadn't seen anyone who didn't look as though they belonged at the party.

I was deep in those thoughts when the door to Nebel's office opened and he stuck his head out. "Jessica, so sorry to keep you waiting. I wasn't expecting you. I'm afraid I'm going to be in this meeting for a while longer." He motioned for Carraway to come to where we sat. "Richard, I've kept Mrs. Fletcher and her friend waiting too long. Do me a favor and take these good folks for something to eat, coffee, whatever."

"No, Senator," I said. "We really don't need to—"

Nebel closed the door in midsentence, leaving Carraway and us to decide what to do. It didn't take me long to make a decision. This was a good opportunity to spend time with the aide, hopefully to learn more about just how deep his negative feelings about Nikki Farlow ran.

"I'd love a cup of tea," I said.

Carraway, who was as pale and nervous as I'd remembered him from the dinner, asked whether we wanted him to have tea or coffee sent up.

"No," I said pleasantly, standing and smiling. "I feel as though we're in the way here. Besides, I could use a walk."

"We'll have to go the cafeteria downstairs," Carraway said. "Staffers don't have privileges in the dining room."

"Sounds good to me," George said.

The cafeteria was immense, brightly lit, and served a wide variety of foods, including hot dishes, a long salad bar, and a deli section where uniformed workers prepared sandwiches, hamburgers, and hot dogs. I placed my cup of tea and a bowl of rice pudding on the tray, alongside George's coffee and slice of key lime pie. Carraway settled for an orange juice.

Once we were at a Formica table, I said, "I'm sure everyone is still upset about what happened this morning."

Carraway managed a grim laugh. "That's an understatement," he said, dabbing at perspiration on his brow and cheeks with a napkin. "That crazy old man could have killed somebody. You really know him from back home?"

"Yes, I do. Oscar Brophy has always been a bit of a mystery in Cabot Cove, an eccentric who lives by himself. He may not have seemed it, but he's an intelligent man, very well-read. I can't justify his actions. The controversy surrounding the nuclear plant obviously caused him to go off the deep end."

"It's a good thing you were there," Carraway said, "to talk him out of it. He might have shot everybody."

"I'm just glad no one was hurt," I said, tasting my rice pudding.

"Any further developments on Ms. Farlow's death?" George asked.

"Do you mean have they found who killed her?" Carraway asked, guffawing. "The answer is no, and I bet they never do."

His reply caused George and me to sit up a little straighter. "Why do you say that?" I asked.

He downed his orange juice in one continuous gulp before answering. "The Fairfax police don't know what they're doing. You don't see a whole lot of murders in Fairfax County. Besides, lots of people wanted Nikki dead."

"Is that so?" George said. "Why would many people want to harm a lovely young woman like that?"

"Nikki was not your nicest person," Carraway said. "You know, one of those overly ambitious women who don't care who they step on to get ahead. She's made lots of enemies since coming to Washington to join Nebel's staff, and you can count me among them."

George started to say something but Carraway cut him off. "Yeah, I know, that makes me a prime suspect. Frankly, I don't care whether I am or not. All I know is that Nikki had it coming, but I didn't do it."

George asked, "Have the police questioned you yet, Mr. Carraway?"

"Tonight," he replied. "Detective Moody, or one of his cops, is coming to my apartment."

"Have others in the office been questioned?" I asked.

"Maybe, maybe not. I don't care about them." His eyebrows went up and he came forward onto his elbows. "Oh,

I see what you're getting at," he said. "If I talk this way to the police, they'll probably lock me up, case closed. Not only did I not like Nikki; I benefit from her death. Senator Nebel is giving me her job, at least until he decides to hire somebody else. Frankly, I don't give a damn about that, either. I hate to rush you, but I really have to get back upstairs. All hell has broken loose around the office, reporters calling, cops in and out, and all this on top of the vote coming up on the Maine power plant."

His mention of the pending Senate vote on the Cabot Cove nuclear facility prompted George to ask, "What role did Ms. Farlow play in the debate over locating the plant in Maine?"

Another shrug from Carraway. "She had the senator's ear, that's for sure."

George pressed: "Whose side was she on?"

Carraway pushed back his chair, indicating that our little get-together was over. He said, "Nikki had strong convictions about a lot of legislation that came through our office. The problem was, her convictions were based upon who had the most money to spread around. Ready to go? I really can't be away any longer."

Quite an accusation, I thought. Could he back it up, or was it simply a nasty charge from someone whose dislike of her seemed to border on hatred?

The authorities with whom Nebel was meeting were on the way out as we arrived back at the suite, and the senator introduced us.

"A pleasure meeting you, Mrs. Fletcher," one of the MPD detectives said. "I've been meaning to contact you about what happened here this morning. We understand the assailant is a friend of yours."

"Not exactly a friend," I corrected, "but I did know him back home in Cabot Cove, Maine. I'll be happy to talk to you any time you wish."

"How about now?"

I looked at George, who nodded his approval. "Okay," I said.

The detective turned to Nebel: "Got a private office we could use, Senator?"

"Of course," Nebel replied, leading us to a cramped room at the rear of the outer office. It was a brief meeting: The detective asked me about Oscar's background, and I told him what I knew, stressing that I doubted whether Oscar really intended to kill the senator, or anyone else, for that matter. Before the meeting broke up, he informed me that I probably would be called as a witness—which I'd already anticipated—and I assured him I would make myself available whenever I was needed.

As I stood to leave, he said, "By the way, Mrs. Fletcher, Mr. Brophy's gun was empty. No ammunition in it."

"I'm pleased to hear that," I said.

"A sharp defense attorney will make good use of it at his trial."

When I returned, George was seated in the senator's office. I poked my head in. "George, I think we'd better be going," I said, realizing we needed to leave enough time to get to the Nebel house in McLean.

"Going to my house, are you?" Nebel said.

"Yes. Detective Moody from the Fairfax police is meeting us there. He said he intended to inform you."

"He did," Nebel said. "The problem is that Pat will be there."

"Really?" I said. "I saw her early this morning at a meeting at the Library of Congress."

"I know," he said, "but she wasn't feeling well and went home. Actually, I'm glad you'll be there. She needs all the support she can get."

We all turned at the sound of Nebel's secretary telling someone that the senator was busy. That didn't stop Congresswoman Gail Marshall-Miner from entering the office. "Oh, sorry," she said at seeing us. To Nebel: "Warren, I have to talk to you."

"We were just leaving," I said.

She ignored us and sat in a chair, shapely legs crossed beneath a short tan skirt.

"I believe you met Mrs. Fletcher and Inspector Sutherland at the house the other night," Nebel said.

"Yes," the congresswoman said. "Warren, I—"

"It was nice seeing you again," I said to Marshall-Miner as we left the office. I didn't say to George what I was thinking—that Nebel and Marshall-Miner seemed to have a relationship beyond mutual political interests. Women seem to have a better-honed sense of such things than men.

But as we headed up the hall, George said casually, "Looks like the senator and the congresslady are quite cozy." So much for my theory.

We'd almost reached the elevators when Sandy Teller, Nebel's press secretary, came running after us.

"Mrs. Fletcher, I think I've convinced Senator Nebel to hold a press conference to head off the allegations that are flying around town," he said. "I'm counting on you to be with him."

"I really don't think that would be appropriate," I said.

"The senator is counting on you, Mrs. Fletcher," Teller said, his tone more a command than a request.

"I'll have to think about it," I said. "Right now, Inspector Sutherland and I are late for an appointment."

"Where are you going?" Teller asked.

"Lunch," George lied, taking my elbow and hustling me away. "Cheeky chap," he said as we rode down in the elevator.

"Self-important, that's for sure," I said.

"There doesn't seem to be a shortage of that in Washington," George said.

"They're all under tremendous pressure," I said. "The senator has found himself in the proverbial kettle of fish."

George chuckled as he said, "Why do I have the feeling we're about to join those fish?"

Chapter Twelve

An encampment of media vehicles, including two TV remote trucks, greeted us as our cab approached the house. They'd been corralled into an area to the side of the access road by a private security guard and uniformed Fairfax County officers. Before being allowed to proceed to the house, we were stopped to verify our identities. While handing an officer my passport (since I don't possess a driver's license, I always carry my passport for identification purposes), I spotted the reporter, Natalie Mumford. She waved at me, called my name, and tried to approach the taxi, but an officer kept her from doing it and we drove away.

Jardine, the houseman, responded to my knocking and escorted us to the large room overlooking the terrace and river, where Detective Moody stood by the window. Standing next to him was the tall, slender, patrician Hal Duncan, Nebel's attorney. They turned at our arrival.

"Lovely day," Duncan said after greetings had been exchanged.

"A tad too warm for my taste," George said.

"Enjoying your stay in Washington?" Moody asked us.

Duncan laughed. "After what happened this morning to Mrs. Fletcher with that madman, I'm sure she has ambivalent feelings about our city."

"It hasn't been boring," I said.

"I would imagine," said Moody. "First a murder here, and then—"

"An *alleged* murder," Duncan corrected.

Moody, who wore a yellow windbreaker over a blue button-down shirt and chinos, said, "The counselor here is with us to make sure no one says anything he doesn't want to hear." His sarcasm wasn't lost on anyone, including Duncan.

"I hardly think that's necessary," I said to the lawyer.

"Just a formality," Duncan said through practiced lockjaw and what was intended to be a reassuring smile. "After all, Ms. Farlow's unfortunate death occurred here at my client's home, who happens to be a United States senator. I think it's appropriate for me to be present when the police question people about it."

"Am I being questioned?" I asked Moody.

"No, ma'am."

"Have you spoken again with Mrs. Nebel?" I asked.

"Is she here?" Moody asked.

"Upstairs resting," Duncan said.

George had drifted away from us and stood in front of the massive fireplace. I wondered what he was thinking, whether he'd had second thoughts about becoming involved through me in a murder investigation. I wouldn't have blamed him; at that moment I was suffering a serious case of second thoughts myself.

I was also resentful of Mr. Duncan's presence, and his stated reason for being there. I had every right to speak with Detective Moody without an attorney present, especially one with whom I had no relationship.

"Detective Moody," I said, "Inspector Sutherland and I came here this afternoon to speak with you. I'm not interested in having Mr. Duncan present."

Duncan scrutinized me for a second, a frown on his brow, before saying with a smile, "I'll be happy to absent myself, Mrs. Fletcher, while you and the good detective have your little talk. But I'll be here in the house in the event you'd like my involvement. I know you're not looking for legal advice, but you might keep in mind that you and your inspector friend were at the dinner party—along with all the other suspects."

"*Suspects?*" George said, incredulous.

Duncan left the room without bothering to elaborate.

"Feel like some fresh air?" Moody asked, his tone blurring the difference between a simple question and an editorial comment about Duncan's presence in the room. "I'd like to go with you down to the dock."

"Fine," I said.

"No need for you to come, Inspector," Moody said.

I answered for George: "I'd like him with us, Detective."

"If you insist."

"I insist."

We went through the doors to the terrace and headed for the wooden staircase. I stopped.

"Something wrong, Jessica?" George asked.

"I don't know," I said, retracing my steps and reentering the house, George and Moody following. I stood in the middle of the room and stared at the fireplace, my eyes focused on the elaborate set of antique brass fireplace tools.

"That's one big fireplace," Moody said. "Probably doesn't get much use. We don't get too much fireplace weather in Virginia."

"But we do in Maine," I said, approaching the tools and bending over to get a closer look. I ran my fingers over the shiny finish on each handle, straightened, and silently counted the tools. By this time, George and Moody had come to my side.

"There's one missing," I said flatly.

"Pardon?" said Moody.

"There's a tool missing," I repeated.

"A fireplace tool?" George asked.

"Yes," I replied. "Look. This wrought-iron stand has a slot for each tool. One of the slots is empty." I faced him and said, "Obviously, if Ms. Farlow was murdered, the killer hit her with something. The gash in the back of her head could have been caused by a fireplace tool."

George moved closer to the tool stand. "The logical one would be a poker," he said. "But that's here." He picked up the poker and held it out for us.

"Logical," I said, "but not necessarily the only tool that could have been used." I did another count of the tools in the stand—a small broom, a shovel for taking ashes out of the fireplace, a brush used to clean the walls and grate, and the poker that George had replaced in the stand.

"I'm no fireplace expert," Moody said, "but it looks to me like those are all the tools anybody would need."

We turned at the sound of a door opening. Jardine, the houseman, entered the room carrying a vase of colorful fresh flowers. He set it on a table and was poised to leave when I said, "Jardine, do you have a minute?"

"Yes, ma'am."

"These fireplace tools," I said. "Do you clean them often?"

His expression said he was concerned I'd found a tool he'd failed to clean properly.

"Yes, ma'am," he said. "Is something wrong?"

"I was wondering whether a tool is missing," I said.

He approached the fireplace and scrutinized the tool rack. "No, ma'am," he said, "I don't think so." His lips twitched, and he ran his tongue over them. His eyes went from person to person.

"Well," I said, "it looks like I'm wrong."

"Is that all?" Jardine asked, backing away from us.

"Yes, thank you."

He crossed the room and was about to go through the door. Instead he stopped, turned, and said in a barely audible voice, "The blow poke."

"The what?" Moody asked.

"The blow poke," Jardine repeated.

"Come over here," Moody said.

When Jardine was again within our circle, Moody asked, "What's this about some blow poke?"

"It isn't here," Jardine muttered.

"What's a blow poke?" Moody asked us.

"A fireplace tool," George answered.

"It's a combination tool," I added. "You can use it to stir the fire, and you can blow through it to provide air to a specific area."

"Come to think of it, I do know what a blow poke is," Moody said. "I watch Court TV with my wife when I get a chance, and they covered a murder trial up in North Carolina a while back. As I recall, something called a blow poke was the murder weapon."

"When did you last see it?" George asked Jardine.

The short, slender houseman shrugged. "I don't know," he said.

Moody grunted. "This blow poke," he said. "It's what, hollow so you can blow through it?"

"Yes," I said. "I have one at home."

"Not solid," Moody said.

"That's right," said George. "I have one, too. It's quite lightweight."

Another grunt from Moody. "That might explain it," he said.

"Explain *what?*" I asked.

"Why there was no brain injury to Ms. Farlow. The autopsy—we got the results just before I came here—the autopsy showed no significant brain injury, no skull fractures. She died strictly from blood loss."

George nodded. "A more solid instrument would likely have inflicted brain injury," he proffered.

Moody realized Jardine was still standing with us. "Thank you," he said, his unmistakable message that the houseman was free to leave. Once he was gone, the detective said, "This is all interesting, but it's pure speculation. Let's go down to the dock, if you don't mind."

We were almost to the door when Patricia Nebel and Hal Duncan entered the room. She looked drawn, her face even thinner than usual. She seemed shocked at seeing us there.

"Hello, Pat," I said.

She avoided me and asked Moody, "Why are *you* here?"

"Didn't your husband tell you I was coming?" he replied. "I spoke with him earlier."

"No, he didn't." To me: "Jessica, what's going on?"

"Detective Moody asked me to meet him here," I said. "Frankly, I'm not sure why." I looked to Moody for an answer.

"Just a routine follow-up," he offered.

"Mrs. Nebel would like all of you to leave," Duncan said.

"Perhaps we should—" George started to say, but Moody interrupted.

"I'm sorry to bother you, ma'am," the detective said, "but now that it's been determined that Ms. Farlow's death was a homicide, I have a need to spend additional time here at the scene. I asked Mrs. Fletcher to join me because I think she might be helpful in the investigation."

"How could you be helpful, Jessica?" Pat asked. "You didn't know anyone at the party. You didn't even know Nikki."

Before I could answer, Moody announced, "We were in the process of going down to the dock when you arrived, Mrs. Nebel. We'll do that now and try not to disturb you any more than necessary." His deep, rich baritone both soothed, yet established his authority.

I turned and asked Pat Nebel, "Was there a blow poke among the fireplace tools, Pat?"

"What?"

"The fireplace tools," I said. "There appears to be one missing. Jardine said it was a blow poke."

"A blow poke?" Pat said. "Yes, there was one, but—"

"Mrs. Nebel has nothing more to say," said Duncan. "She's not been well and—"

"I'm quite capable of speaking for myself," Pat said, her tone causing the attorney to stiffen, his mouth a taut, straight line. "That tool set was a gift from Christine."

"Your daughter?" Moody asked.

"Yes." Pat went to the stand holding the tools, examined its contents, turned, and said, "You're right. The blow poke is missing."

"When did you last see it?" I asked.

"Please," Duncan said, coming to Pat's side and placing his hand on her arm as though to physically move her away. "I must insist that—"

"Shut up, Hal!" Pat said. "You may speak for Warren, but you don't speak for me. I saw that tool only a few days ago. A visitor admired the set. It's very unusual, an original designed by a Maine craftsman and artist. My visitor had never seen a blow poke before and took it out of the stand."

"A few days ago?" George said.

"Yes. I can't imagine why it's not here now. My friend replaced it after looking at it."

"Who was this friend?" Moody asked.

"Jean Watson. She's on my literacy committee. Her husband, Jack, is a veterinarian. They're neighbors."

Moody jotted the name in a notebook and turned to me. "Coming?" he asked.

George and I walked away from Patricia and Duncan and followed the detective out to the terrace, pausing at the head of the stairs leading down to the dock.

"I have the feeling you asked us here for more than just a talk," I told the detective.

He looked back at the house before saying, "I want your help."

"What help could I possibly be?" I asked.

"You're close to the Nebel family—and you don't have any ax to grind, Mrs. Fletcher."

"That may be true, Detective, but I'm afraid my friendship with Patricia Nebel is the extent of it. And we're not particularly close. I barely know the senator."

Another glance at the house. "You know about the senator's affair with the deceased."

I glanced at George before replying, "I've heard the rumors like everyone else, but I don't have any firsthand information."

"Let's go down," he said.

When we reached the dock, Moody said, "I'll level with you, Mrs. Fletcher. We don't get a lot of murders here in Fairfax County. This is maybe my second or third murder investigation, and I've been on the force for twenty-six years." He grinned broadly, his teeth a bright white against the blackness of his skin. "And I sure never thought I'd be looking at a United States senator as the prime suspect."

"Isn't that a trifle premature, Detective?" George said.

Moody reacted to George's voice as though he'd forgotten he was there. "That's right," he said. "You're a Scotland Yard inspector, probably handled hundreds of homicides."

"I've had my share," George said.

"Yeah, well, I haven't—had my share." He faced George, hands on hips. "Ever handled a murder investigation where the president of England sticks his nose in it?"

"The president?" George said. "We have a prime minister."

"Whatever. Look, the chief gets a call from somebody in President Dimond's office. It seems the president—he's the same party as Senator Nebel—the president doesn't want the senator involved with this. My boss says the Senate is almost fifty-fifty Republicans and Democrats, and if Nebel loses his seat, the other side picks it up. In other words, my boss, who happens to be a political animal, doesn't want the senator to be the one who killed Ms. Farlow. Am I making sense?"

"I'm sure the senator would agree," George said.

"So," Moody said, "it's to my advantage to clear the senator."

"As opposed to finding out who killed Nikki Farlow?" I said, unable to disguise my disappointment with his message.

"I deserved that," Moody said, "but cut me some slack. You spent time with the victim, Mrs. Fletcher. Did she say anything that might point to someone at the party who didn't like her, somebody she might have been afraid of?"

"No," I answered.

"Inspector?"

"I was with Mrs. Fletcher all evening," he said. "I saw, and heard, what she saw and heard."

Moody pulled a piece of paper from his yellow windbreaker and consulted it. "My wife says you probably make lists when you're writing your murder mysteries," he said. "You know, suspect lists, motives, maybe even make charts to keep things straight."

I glanced at George, whose expression was bemusement.

"So," said Moody, "I made a list of my own—of suspects. I figure maybe you saw something with one of these people at the dinner party, maybe overheard something one of them said."

"Detective," I said, "I really don't think that—"

"My wife says mystery writers have a really keen nose for things like that. And here you were at the party with a real Scotland Yard inspector. Between the two of you, I figured—"

George's cell phone rang. He removed it from his pocket and walked away from us. When he returned, he said, "I'm afraid I must leave immediately. There's been a terrorist incident in London—two people killed, many wounded, I'm told—and I'm needed."

"You're going back to London?" I said, disappointment obvious in my voice.

"No," he said. "We've set up an operations center here in Washington. I'll be there to help coordinate things back home. I'm sure someone up at the house will fetch me a taxi."

"Forget it," said Moody, yanking a two-way radio from his belt. "One of my men will take you wherever you want to go. Least I can do for a fellow lawman. Hands across the sea, huh?"

"I appreciate that," George said. While Moody made his call, George kissed me, gave my arms a squeeze, told me he'd call that evening, and went up the stairs two at a time.

The sound of a boat's motor caused us to turn. Jack Nebel deftly maneuvered the Aquasport to the dock, tilted the Evinrude out of the water, expertly secured its lines to the cleats on the dock, and jumped out.

"Hello," I said.

"Hello," he replied, walking past us. "I'm late." He hurried up the steps. I noted that this time he took the ignition key with him.

"Detective Moody," I said, "I assured you that I would do anything I could to help in your investigation. I meant that. But you're asking me to tell you what people said, or did, and I'm uncomfortable passing along hearsay." I was thinking specifically of what Pat Nebel had told me. If she'd revealed something tangible, some specific piece of hard evidence, I would have immediately passed that along to Moody. But what she'd said was based on pure speculation—except, I amended my thought, for having overheard the conversation about Nikki Farlow's blackmailing of Senator Nebel. I drew a breath and was about to tell him of that conversation when he saved me the trouble.

"The deceased, Ms. Farlow, was blackmailing the senator," he said matter-of-factly.

I said nothing, hoping my surprise at his knowing what I already knew wasn't obvious.

"Pretty strong motive, huh?"

"If it's true. This city seems to be fueled by such rumors."

"More than a rumor, ma'am. We have a letter she sent him about it."

"Oh," was all I could muster. "Where did you get it?"

"Not really at liberty to say, Mrs. Fletcher."

"I understand," I said. What I wanted to say was that I would love to see the letter. I decided there was nothing to be lost by asking—and did.

To my amazement, he said, "Sure." He pulled an eight-by-ten sheet of white paper, folded in thirds, from his jacket pocket and handed it to me. "It's a photocopy," he said.

"May I take this with me?" I asked.

"Afraid not," he said. "Sorry."

Why is he allowing me to see the letter? I wondered as I unfolded the paper and read what was on it. I handed it back to him.

"Interesting, huh?" he said.

I nodded. My mind raced. I was frantically chewing on what I'd just read when he said, "I'd like to go over a couple of names with you, people who were at the party."

"All right," I said, wanting to ask to see the letter again—to commit it to memory—but reluctant. "Where do you want to start?"

"How about the two members of Congress who were here, Ms. Marshall-Miner and Mr. Barzelouski?"

The only two people mentioned by name in the letter I'd just read.

Chapter Thirteen

Once we'd finished discussing names on Moody's list, and before I left him alone on the dock to return to the house to spend a few minutes with Pat Nebel, I told him of my observations about the Aquasport—that the engine was warm, indicating it had been used during the time the party was in progress; the black shoe marks on the terrace and a few of the steps; that the key had been left in the ignition; the oil leak in the outboard engine; and that whoever used it during the party was either a rank amateur sailor, or had been in a great hurry, judging from the engine's being left in the water, and the slipshod way the boat had been tethered to the dock. He thanked me for the information, and requested that I not discuss the letter he'd shown me with anyone, something I expected him to do before handing it to me. I assured him, of course, that I would honor his request.

We said good-bye, and I went up to the house, leaving

him to take a closer look at the Aquasport. Jardine was there when I arrived. He informed me that Mrs. Nebel wasn't feeling well and didn't wish to be disturbed. Whether she was physically ill or wilting under the pressures of the past few days was impossible to determine. All I knew was that she was keeping a low profile, which was probably smart. What her absences would mean to the success of the literacy initiative was conjecture. Chances were that she'd done all her important work ahead of time, and any appearances would be purely symbolic.

Jardine turned to leave, but I called his name.

"Yes, ma'am?"

I was curious about the boat down at the dock," I said. "The Aquasport."

"Yes, ma'am?"

"Who uses it?"

"The family," he replied.

"Everyone in the family?"

"Yes, ma'am. Jack mostly."

"I see. Jardine, do you ever use the boat?"

"Oh, no, ma'am. I wouldn't know how."

His response didn't satisfy me. I wanted to ask further questions, but he said he had an important chore to do, and excused himself.

"I need a taxi," I said.

"I will call one for you, ma'am."

While waiting for a taxi to arrive, I called George's cell phone.

"Sutherland here," he said.

"It's Jessica. I'm just leaving the house."

"Fruitful?" he asked.

"Yes, as a matter of fact," I said, thinking of the letter shown me by Detective Moody. "I haven't had a chance to catch up on the news. The terrorist attack?"

"Worse than originally reported, I'm afraid. Five dead and scores injured. I'll be late into the evening. I suggested returning to London, but my superior dissuaded me."

I was pleased to hear that, but didn't express it. Instead I said, "I suppose dinner is out."

"Afraid so, my dear, much to my regret. Unless, of course—"

"Don't give it even a second thought," I said. "What you're doing is far more important than any dinner. Call me on my cell when, and if, you get a breather."

"Shall do. Till later."

I told the cabdriver to take me to the Willard, but as we approached the hotel I had a change of mind. I'd asked Detective Moody for Nikki Farlow's address in Washington, and he'd given it to me, saying that the Washington MPD, working in concert with the Fairfax County police, had already searched her apartment in the Capitol Hill area. "Her parents are here from Ohio," he'd added. "Sad reason for a trip to Washington."

I gave the driver Nikki's address, and he delivered me to a pretty, tree-lined street a few blocks from the Capitol Building. I checked numbers on the doors, found Nikki's, and rang the bell next to her name on a listing of tenants in the foyer. A male voice said, "Who is it?"

"My name is Jessica Fletcher," I responded. "I was a . . . I was friendly with Nikki."

"Just a moment." He came back on the intercom a few seconds later and said, "Jessica Fletcher, the mystery writer?"

"Yes."

"You and Nikki were friends?"

"Not exactly, but we had met and spent some time together."

I didn't know what to say next, because I wasn't sure why I'd even come there. The man spared me further explanation by saying, "Please come up."

The door leading from the small foyer to the building's interior was buzzed open, and I soon found myself standing in Nikki's second-floor apartment, where her father and mother, Greg and Charlotte Farlow, greeted me.

"I'm so sorry for your loss," I said after introductions.

"It's the worst thing a parent can face," said her mother, "outliving your child."

I agreed, and accepted their offer to sit with them in the pretty, sunny kitchen.

"Nikki never mentioned knowing you," her father, a tall, heavy man with a head of tousled white hair and a ruddy face, said.

"We'd just recently become acquainted," I said. "I didn't know your daughter well, but I was impressed with her. She seemed such an organized, capable young woman."

Charlotte cried, which I was sure she'd done a hundred times since receiving news of her daughter's demise. She wiped her eyes with a pretty embroidered handkerchief. "Murdered!" she said flatly, bewildered. "How can it be?"

"Nikki always dismissed danger, Mrs. Fletcher," Greg Farlow said, "at least where it concerned her." He shook his head. "She was fatalistic about danger. If it happened, it happened, was the way she viewed it."

Charlotte, as tall as her husband but considerably slimmer, managed a small smile. "I bet you'd like a cup of tea, Mrs. Fletcher," she said.

"Oh, please, I don't—"

"It won't be any trouble," she said. "I ran across tea bags a few minutes ago. Nikki was always so organized. I suppose that's why she was successful in business."

"She told me she'd had a placement firm in Chicago," I said.

"Yes," the father said. "Built it from scratch into a thriving business. I suppose that was one reason Senator Nebel asked her to join his staff here in Washington. I suggested she turn him down, but working in Congress was the sort of challenge Nikki couldn't resist."

I thought of the rumor that their daughter and the senator had been engaged in an affair, and wondered how much they knew about it. I didn't have to wait long to find out. As Nikki's mother placed a steaming cup in front of me, she said, "It's hard enough having your only child murdered in the prime of her life, but to hear these vicious rumors about her and the senator only rubs salt into the wound."

"I can imagine the additional pain it's caused you," I said. I hesitated before asking, "Did Nikki ever talk about it with you?"

"Some," George said. "We knew how ludicrous it was."

Terming it *ludicrous* surprised me. While I understood why a parent would want to dismiss such a salacious charge against a beloved daughter, it certainly couldn't have been ruled out of the question. Senator Nebel's reputation was that of a man with an eye for women outside his marriage, and Nikki was an attractive woman. They worked in close proximity, undoubtedly spending many long hours together. That they might have entered into an affair didn't seem ludicrous to me.

"How well did you know Nikki?" her father asked me.

"As I said, not well at all. We corresponded about my trip to Washington, and we spoke on the phone a few times. I really only met her in person the day she died."

"Then you probably didn't know," said Mr. Farlow.

"I don't think it's necessary to go into this, Greg," Charlotte said.

"Why not?" he replied. "Nikki was never embarrassed about it, nor were we."

I took in each of them, hoping for an explanation. It came from Nikki's father.

"Nikki was a lesbian," he said, checking his wife for an angry reaction.

She looked down at the table, then up at me. "I was upset at first when she told us, Mrs. Fletcher, as I'm sure you can understand." Her smile was more of a grimace. "Funny what goes through your mind at a time like that. My immediate thought was a selfish one—that I'd never have grandchildren." Tears ran down her cheeks. "I wasn't thinking of Nikki. I was thinking only of me."

"That's understandable," I said. But my mind was racing.

Any affair between Nebel and Nikki was highly unlikely—unless Nikki had magically become heterosexual—and the blackmailing Pat Nebel spoke of didn't make any sense.

"I don't mean to pry," I said. "But I have to admit to you that I've taken it upon myself to assist the authorities in helping identify Nikki's murderer, and bringing him—or her—to justice. That's why I came here today."

Mr. Farlow said, "I know you write murder mysteries, Mrs. Fletcher, but I didn't know you worked with the police to solve real ones, too."

"I'm not an official investigator," I said, not wanting to give them the wrong impression. "Was your daughter's sexual orientation known to others? I mean, to a wide range of friends and colleagues here in Washington?"

"Oh, no," her mother answered. "It wasn't that Nikki was ashamed. Far from it. And you must know that we weren't ashamed, either. Once the initial shock was over, we supported her fully. But did her friends know? A few back home, that's all, and Nikki told us she kept it a secret here in Washington, again not because of any embarrassment, but because she felt it might hamper her work in the Senate. It pained her to be the subject of the rumors about her and Senator Nebel. She could have put an end to them in an instant by publicly announcing that she was a lesbian. But she never did, just discussed it with us whenever she came home, or when we visited her here."

"Actually, Nikki found the whole situation amusing," said her father. "I remember once when she expressed concern about how the rumor could negatively affect his run for a third term. I suggested that if she was seriously worried about that, that she make her lesbianism public."

"What did she say?" I asked.

"She said that she'd discussed it with Senator Nebel, and that he urged her not to for her own sake."

"Then Senator Nebel knew," I said.

"Yes," they answered in unison.

I tried to keep up with my racing thoughts. If the senator knew that Nikki was a lesbian, he could have headed off the rumors about their affair by leaking that fact—and Washington's penchant for leaks to the press was well-known. If Greg Farlow was correct that his daughter had confided in Senator Nebel about her sexual orientation, why had Nebel not used it to quash the rumor? Was it simply the honorable act of an honorable man, who placed loyalty to his aide above his political future? That was the most palatable of reasons. Then again, something more nefarious could have been behind it. The person who knew the answer was Senator Warren Nebel. But I didn't know if he would ever be willing to shed light on it.

I asked Greg and Charlotte, "Did Nikki have a partner here in Washington?"

"A romantic interest?" her mother said. "I don't believe so. At least, she never told me about one. I would have liked her to develop a relationship, someone she could love." A few more silent tears flowed.

"Did she ever mention anyone she considered an enemy, someone who might have hated her enough to want to kill her?" I asked.

Her parents looked at each other before her father

said, "Nikki often spoke of how intense things were in Washington between opposing sides on an issue. She—"

"She talked about how hatred sometimes developed between political rivals," the mother said. "In fact—"

Greg Farlow jumped in: "Nikki told me that there were people in Washington who hated Senator Nebel, and carried that feeling over to anyone who supported him and believed in his politics."

Which meant there might have been a few hundred individuals in Washington who carried a grudge against her, I thought.

Charlotte added, "Nikki sometimes spoke of the corruption that's rampant in Washington, payoffs to politicians from lobbyists, under-the-table deals, things like that. Not that everyone here operates that way. She was always quick to point that out. But she hated corruption and dishonesty, truly detested it."

"Was she intimately involved with legislation?" I asked. "I assume she would be, being a senator's top aide."

"Oh, yes. Nikki had a keen interest in legislation. She was passionate about certain issues," Charlotte said.

I hesitated before asking, "What about Senator Nebel? Did she ever say he was among the corrupt?"

They looked at each other. Greg answered, "I don't remember her ever mentioning Senator Nebel in that regard." His wife agreed.

I sensed I'd intruded on them long enough, and got up from the table. "Will you be staying in Washington long?" I asked.

"We'd hoped to bring Nikki back with us for burial," said the mother. "But the police told us that because it's a homicide, her body won't be released for a while. Whether we stay depends upon how long that will be."

"Of course," I said. "Where are you staying?"

"Capitol Hill Suites. It's very nice, and not too expensive. We thought of staying here at the apartment, but . . ."

"I plan to be here for the week," I said. "I'd like to stay in touch."

"Sure," Greg Farlow said. "It was good of you to come by, and to be taking an interest in Nikki's case."

I left the building with my brain swirling with questions and emotions. Nikki's parents were lovely people. Their acceptance of their daughter's sexual orientation was admirable, as was their strength in dealing with her premature death.

But uppermost in my mind as I walked away from the building was the revelation that Nikki was homosexual, hardly interested in an affair with a male United States senator. Nebel knew that about her, yet did nothing to use that knowledge to put an end to rumors of an affair with her. He'd obviously not even confided in his wife that her suspicions about Nikki and him were groundless. Why?

If I'd developed an interest earlier in helping solve Nikki Farlow's murder, that interest was now intensified. I stopped at a corner, pulled out my cell phone and Walter Grusin's business card from my purse, and dialed his number.

"Mr. Grusin? Jessica Fletcher."

"I was hoping to hear from you."

"I decided to take you up on your offer to fill me in on the nuclear power plant. The more I know about it, from all sides, the better."

"An enlightened view, Mrs. Fletcher. I'm at your disposal. How about dinner?"

"Dinner?" Spending an evening having dinner with him wasn't high on my priority list. But if that was when he was available, it would have to be.

"I happen to be free this evening," I said, wishing that weren't the case.

"Any druthers about a restaurant?" he asked.

"I'm a visitor," I said. "This is your town."

"I'll do my best to make this visitor happy. Where can I meet you?"

"The Willard? I'm staying there and need some time to freshen up."

"Two hours?"

"I look forward to it."

Chapter Fourteen

I turned on the television in my suite at the Willard the moment I walked in and saw what George was dealing with, an unconscionable terrorist attack at a bus stop in central London. The footage of the aftermath was sickening; no terrorist group had yet claimed responsibility for the cowardly act.

The newspaper reporter, Natalie Mumford, and Senator Nebel's press secretary, Sandy Teller, had called. I returned Teller's call first and reached him at his office in the senator's Dirksen Building suite.

"Thanks for getting back to me," he said. "I'd mentioned to you that I've been urging the senator to hold a press conference about Nikki's death. I think he's finally agreed with me."

"I'm sure that pleases you," I said.

"I just know it's the right thing to do. The problem is that his lawyer, Hal Duncan, is against it."

Of course he is, I thought. Nebel was obviously a prime suspect in Nikki's murder, and every attorney knows that in a criminal case, the less said by a client, the better.

"Why are you telling *me* this?" I asked.

"I was hoping you could persuade the senator to follow my advice and override Duncan."

"Mr. Teller," I said, "I'm afraid you have a mistaken notion of my relationship with Senator Nebel. I'm a friend of his wife's, not his. He wouldn't have reason to heed any advice I might give."

"You underestimate yourself, Mrs. Fletcher. He's been expressing his admiration for you every chance he gets."

"That's all very flattering, but I'm not in a position to give counsel to anyone when it comes to press conferences, especially since the senator's attorney—who, I might add, seems extremely capable—feels otherwise."

"Well, Mrs. Fletcher, I had nothing to lose by asking, and I understand why you feel the way you do. How did your meeting with Detective Moody go this afternoon out at the house?"

Another attempt by this press secretary to a United States senator to find out through me what's going on. I suppose I couldn't blame him. His responsibility, besides putting a positive spin on his boss's agenda in the senate, included keeping tabs on things that could prove detrimental.

"It went fine," I said, wondering how much he knew about the alleged blackmail attempt by Nikki, and the revelation that her sexual orientation rendered an affair with the senator unlikely. My assumption was that while he might have been brought into the loop where the blackmail was involved, I doubted he knew of Nikki's lesbianism. If he did, I couldn't imagine his not leaking it to media confidants.

I didn't have to return Natalie Mumford's call, because she called immediately after I'd hung up with Teller.

"Hope I'm not intruding on anything special," she said.

"Not at all," I said.

"I saw you when you arrived at Senator Nebel's house this afternoon. You were there at the same time as Detective Moody."

"That's right," I said.

"And Nebel's attorney, Hal Duncan."

"Right again."

"Mind if I ask what's new with the investigation?"

"I don't mind your asking," I said, "but I'm sure you know a great deal more than I do."

"You may think that, Mrs. Fletcher, but you're probably wrong. Let me ask you a direct question. You know, of course, about Nikki Farlow's supposed affair with the senator."

Her use of the word *supposed* surprised me. When we'd met for that brief time at the restaurant, she'd presented the affair as a fait accompli, a fact.

"I've heard the rumor," I replied.

"Here's another . . . rumor."

I waited.

"Would it surprise you that Nikki was gay?"

This time my silence was because I was dumbfounded. I'd been told this by Nikki's parents just an hour earlier, and here was a reporter demonstrating the same knowledge.

"What do you base that on?" I asked.

"A call to a friend in the Midwest, who did some digging for me. I'd heard something along those lines here in D.C."

"I see."

"I thought you might have some information to help me corroborate it."

"I'm afraid I can't help you there, Ms. Mumford."

"But if in your time with the Nebels you come up with something, you will let me know—won't you?"

"Certainly not," I said, working to keep the indignation out of my voice.

She laughed. "I know, I'm pushy. But that goes with the territory. Actually, if it's true, it would be good for the senator, put to rest the rumor that he and Nikki were having an affair."

But not especially good for Nikki Farlow. She'd wanted to keep her sexual life private from others in Washington, and deserved that respect in death. So did her parents.

I ended the conversation and spruced up for dinner with Walter Grusin. He called from the lobby, and I was almost out the door when the phone rang. I debated letting the answering system pick it up, but succumbed to my need to respond to a ringing telephone.

"Jessica? It's Seth."

"Oh, hello, Seth. How are you?"

"I'm more interested in your welfare at the moment."

"My welfare? Why do you say that?"

"Seems like a silly question to be askin' me, Jessica, considering all that's happened to you in the few days you've been in Washington. First Oscar Brophy shows up wavin' a gun around like the demented old fool that he is, and you end up in his sights. Then—and you never mentioned it to me last time we talked—then this aide to Senator Nebel is found murdered, and Jessica Fletcher happens to be the one who discovers the body—in the company of your Scotland Yard friend, I might add."

"Actually, the aide's murder—her name was Nikki Farlow—her murder happened before Oscar showed up with his gun."

"Doesn't matter what order they came in, Jessica. Point is, you've found yourself in one dangerous situation after another. Not the first time. Maybe you should consider writin' romance novels or kids' books 'stead of murder mysteries."

"I don't think the books I write have anything to do with what's happened since I got here."

"Be that as it may, Jessica, you've landed yourself in a dangerous situation."

I started to respond, but he continued: "I know you've got Mr. Sutherland there at your side, but I wouldn't count on him alone to keep you safe."

I had to smile. Although Seth had been courteous and friendly the few times he'd met George, I was aware of a certain edge on Seth's part, the reason for it escaping me. Did I dare think it was jealousy at George's having entered my life and occupying some of my time and thoughts? I hoped not. I treasured my long friendship with Seth, and would hate to see anything taint it.

"Seth," I said, "it's so good of you to call, and I hate to cut our conversation short, but someone is waiting downstairs in the lobby for me."

"Who might that be? Mr. Sutherland?"

"As a matter of fact, it isn't. George is very busy because of the terrorist attack in London today."

"Ayuh. Saw it on the TV. Whole world's goin' to hell in a handbasket, including Washington."

"Be that as it may, Seth, I really must run. It was good of you to call. I'll keep in touch."

"What time will you be getting back tonight from— Where is it you're goin'?"

"I'm going to dinner with someone, Seth. A friend I've made here."

"Got something to do with the murder?"

"Ah, no."

"Have time when you get back for a nightcap?"

"What?"

"Buy you a nightcap?"

"You're . . . ?"

"Ayuh. I am right here in Washington, D.C., Jessica, in the Willard Hotel. Fancy place."

"Seth, I know that you're concerned about me, and I appreciate that. I truly do. But have you noticed that I'm all grown up now, and—"

"Now, now, Jessica, don't be getting on your high horse. And don't think I came all the way down here to Washington just to keep an eye on you. Fact is, I intend to visit with a doctor friend of mine over at the National Institutes of Health. A fine fella doing some very impressive research."

"I'm glad to hear that," I said.

"I'll be visitin' him tomorrow. Meantime, I'm in room six-twelve. Intend to have some dinner here in the hotel and watch the ball game. So you go on and enjoy your dinner. I'll be here waitin' for your call when you get back."

Chapter Fifteen

Walter Grusin enthusiastically greeted me in the lobby.

"Sorry I took so long," I said. "The phone rang as I was walking out the door."

"Not a problem," he said. "Like Italian food?"

"Very much."

"Great. My particular favorite in Washington is i Ricchi, on Nineteenth. It's Tuscan. They make the best bread in town."

"Sounds wonderful."

He'd parked his car directly in front of the hotel. After a tip to the doorman for keeping his eye on it, we drove to the restaurant, where Grusin was greeted warmly by name and led to a relatively quiet table in the busy, bustling establishment, decorated with terra-cotta tiles, cream-colored archways, and large floral frescoes.

"The usual, Mr. Grusin?" the maître d' asked.

"Please. Jessica?"

"A glass of white wine. Chardonnay?"

"A lady after my own heart," Grusin said. "I drink chardonnay during the week, martinis on the weekend, unless I'm out during the week with clients or politicians. When in Rome . . ."

I remembered back to the ill-fated Nebel dinner party, when I'd noticed Grusin order a chardonnay at the bar.

"I had the impression that alcohol wasn't alien to most of the guests at the party," I said lightly.

He laughed heartily. "Lots of drinking goes on in Washington, Jessica. You don't mind if I call you Jessica, do you? Politics and booze seem to go together. Of course, there are newcomers who bring with them their love affair with bottled water, tofu, and sprouts. But the old-liners stick to their bourbon and gin."

Our wine was served, and Grusin held out his glass. "To a pleasant evening, Jessica Fletcher. I was beginning to believe you when you said you wouldn't have time for me."

"I spoke too soon," I said. "But I decided that since the nuclear power plant might well end up in my backyard, it made sense to learn all I can about it. You seem to be the primary source."

"That's flattering," he said, "and I hope I can put your fears about the plant to rest."

I took in others in i Ricchi. It was obviously an expensive restaurant, popular with the expense-account crowd—lobbyists and politicians—this lobbyist and a writer of murder mysteries. I suppose I should have felt important, being wined and dined like a politician, but I didn't. I was there under false pretenses, pretending to be interested in learning about Sterling Power and the nuclear plant it intended to build in Cabot Cove. The truth was, I was there because I wanted to pump my host about what he knew about Nikki Farlow and her murder. As that thought moved in and out of my mind, it struck me that I might be having dinner with her murderer—unlikely, of course, but possible.

"So," he said, "tell me all about Jessica Fletcher."

"Maybe we should look at a menu before I do that," I said. "To be honest, I'm famished."

"Then that's what we'll do." He motioned to a waiter who'd been hovering nearby.

Orders placed—skewered shrimp for me, a house specialty pasta for him, and soup for both of us—I tried to get him to talk about himself, but he kept shifting the conversation back to me. I wasn't sure whether he did that because he was truly interested, or was practicing a learned conversational gambit. Either way, I decided to go along with him for a while and talked of my early years as a teacher, how I got started as a writer of crime novels, and other aspects of my life that I found interesting, but doubted whether many other people would. I was grateful when our meals arrived, interrupting my monologue. Grusin was right; the homemade bread was heavenly.

A few times during dinner, men and women stopped by to say hello to my host. At one point after two of them had left, I said, "You're a popular fellow."

"I hope so," he said with a pleasant, easy laugh. "An

unpopular lobbyist is like a blind boxer, doomed to fail. Ready for a lecture on why the Sterling Power Company's plan to build a nuclear plant near Cabot Cove makes sense?"

"I'm all ears," I said.

Although I was certain his minilecture had been given to others many times before, he presented it as though it were spontaneous, customizing it to make it personal to me. It was a compelling, well-shaped argument in favor of the power plant, and I listened with intense interest.

"Any questions?" he asked when he was finished.

"I'm sure I'll have many," I said, "but none at this moment. What I'm thinking is how difficult it must be for a politician like Senator Nebel to make important decisions that impact so many people."

"I agree," Grusin said. "People have negative views of us lobbyists, but we serve an important purpose. We help get the facts to elected officials to help them make difficult decisions."

Self-serving facts, I silently added.

"Do you work with Senate staff much?" I asked.

"Depends. Most senators and House members designate someone to be the point man on a given issue, like the power plant."

"Was Nikki Farlow the point man—the point *woman*—on the power plant project?" I asked.

"No," Grusin said. "Carraway is."

"Hmmm."

"You look surprised," he said.

"Oh, no. It's just that I assumed a senator's chief of

staff would be intimately involved in something so important."

He shook his head. "Nikki ran things for Nebel, but that didn't include many legislative matters. She was more an administrator."

"So sad," I said.

"Her death? Yeah, it sure was. They say it was murder. You buy that?"

"I see no reason not to."

"Seems like an accident to me."

"What do you base that on?" I asked. "Did you know her well?"

"Barely knew her at all. My dealings were almost exclusively with Carraway." He looked around the restaurant, leaned close to my ear, and said, "If Nikki *was* murdered, I'd vote for Carraway."

"Oh?"

"Yeah. He's a strange duck. I know one thing: He didn't carry any brief for her."

I nodded. "I gathered the same thing from the few conversations I've had with him. Did you see anything the night of the party that was suspicious?"

"Suspicious? No. I was having too good a time to look for anything like that."

"Someone took the Nebel family boat during the party, probably during dinner. Did you hear it at all?"

"No again. You sound like you're investigating the murder—if that's what it was—along with the police."

I laughed. "No, just the natural curiosity of a mystery writer. Mind if I display that curiosity with you again?"

"Shoot."

"Senator Nebel invited two members of the House of Representatives to his party, the congresswoman from California, Ms. Marshall-Miner, and the Ohio congressman, Mr. Barzelouski."

"Barzelouski!" Grusin said with a chuckle. "The madman of the House of Representatives."

"He does seem volatile. I've seen him speak on occasion on C-SPAN. A fiery orator. I admit to being a neophyte when it comes to politics, but was wondering why certain politicians end up friends. I mean, why would someone like Congressman Barzelouski be invited to Senator Nebel's home for a dinner party celebrating a national literacy drive?"

"Purely politics," Grusin replied. "As off-the-wall as he can be, Barzelouski chairs the House Energy Committee. I'll level with you: I urged Nebel to invite him."

"I suppose my next question is why?"

"Again, purely politics. Barzelouski supports putting the power plant in Cabot Cove, and I thought it was a good opportunity to get him together with Nebel outside Congress. I convinced Barzelouski to champion the literacy program in the House, which endeared him to Nebel."

Obviously the man sitting across from me at the table was good at choreographing relationships to suit his own purposes.

"What about Ms. Marshall-Miner?" I asked.

His response was a low rumble of a laugh, dripping with meaning. He waved for the waiter, who brought dessert menus.

"Not for me," I said. "Coffee would be nice."

While waiting for our coffees, Grusin added a few additional facts to his presentation of why locating the power plant in Cabot Cove would be good for the area's economy, and generate plenty of jobs. I was impressed with his knowledge of where I live, the median income of residents, the pattern of economic growth over the past ten years, the educational level of the town's citizens, and the array and number of jobs the plant would produce. We drank our coffee, and a check was presented to Grusin, a house account that he signed with a flourish.

"Mind another question?" I asked.

"About the power plant?"

"No, about Nikki Farlow."

"Sure you're not working undercover for the Fairfax police?"

"You have my word."

"That's good enough for me."

"I wondered why an attractive, bright, and capable woman like Ms. Farlow never married." Of course, I already knew the answer, but wanted to see what he knew about her sexual orientation.

"Never found the right guy, I suppose," he said. "I really wouldn't know. Ready to call it a night?"

"Yes."

"This was a nice surprise, having dinner with you," he said as we prepared to leave. "I hope my little spiel didn't bore you, and I hope even more that I can count on your support."

"Bored?" I said. "Hardly. I found it fascinating. My support? I'll have to think about that."

"Well," he said, "if you do decide the plant is a good thing for Cabot Cove—and all of Maine, for that matter— I'd appreciate your sharing with Senator Nebel how you feel."

"All right."

"And maybe you'll pass along those feelings to the good folks back home who haven't made up their minds."

We got into his car and he drove me to the Willard. I'd forgotten during the evening that Seth would be waiting for me, and while his unexpected arrival had earlier bothered me, I now looked forward to seeing an old and dear friend.

"Thanks for dinner," I told Grusin as the doorman opened my door.

"The pleasure was all mine," he said.

I was about to step from the car when I turned and said, "When I asked why Congresswoman Marshall-Miner had been invited to Senator Nebel's party, your only response was to laugh."

"Was it?" he said. "Well, let's just say that when it comes to Congresswoman Marshall-Miner and Senator Nebel, the less said the better. Thanks for lending an ear tonight, Jessica. Love to do it again sometime."

Chapter Sixteen

Seth was sitting in the Willard's lobby reading a newspaper when I walked in. He struggled to get out of the large, comfortable chair, his arthritis in evidence, and I reached him before he stood. I leaned over and kissed his cheek.

"You *are* here," I said.

"Ayuh, I certainly am, Jessica. Pleasant evening?"

"Yes, pleasant enough, and interesting, although I'm not sure why."

He pushed himself to his feet and said, "Nightcap? The bar is right elegant."

"I know. I was there last night."

"Seems like you've been doin' your share of ramming since you got here to D.C.," he said as we headed for the Round Robin Bar.

I laughed at his use of the Maine colloquialism for

being out on the town. "Yes, I have been"—I slipped in the Maine phrase for being busy—"all drove up."

I took his arm as we entered the bar and were directed to one of only a few available tables. Seth, who was a moderate drinker—although he has always enjoyed his Manhattans and ward eights—had recently developed a taste for imported beers, and ordered one. I was thirsty and asked for a sparkling water with a wedge of lemon.

"So," he said, settling back, his hands on his corpulent stomach, "tell me about Oscar Brophy, and this lady who was murdered, the senator's assistant."

"I'm sure you know as much as I do about Oscar from reading the papers. I've been told I might have to come back to testify at his trial. Other than that, I've heard nothing. Oh, by the way, he didn't have any bullets in the gun."

"Glad to hear that. I assume he's got a lawyer."

"He'll undoubtedly be appointed one."

"I'll want to speak with whoever that might be."

"Why?"

"I don't think I'm violating the doctor-patient privilege, speakin' with you, Jessica. I know it'll stay right here in this room."

"Go on."

"I've been treatin' Oscar for over a year now for his depression. Severe depression. Every time he came to my office, he'd go off on a rant about the senator and the power plant. Truth is, I should have recognized he was about to go off the deep end and had become even more quee-uh than anybody realized. Might be that an insanity defense is in order for poor old Oscar."

"You should offer that information to whoever represents him. But don't blame yourself, Seth. No one could have foreseen Oscar doing something this drastic. I wonder how he managed to get into that Senate office building carrying a gun. Security seems pretty tight there."

"Sounds like somebody fell down on the job. Now, Jessica, what about this Nikki lady?"

I knew I could count on Seth's discretion, and told him everything I knew— which wasn't that much—and everything I was thinking, which took considerably more time. He listened passively, taking small sips of beer, and occasionally muttering his understanding of what I said. When I was finished with my recounting of events since arriving in Washington, he dabbed at his mouth with his napkin, muffled a discreet burp behind it, and said, "Want my advice?"

"You know your advice is always welcome, Seth."

"My advice, Jessica Fletcher, is to spend what time you have left here promoting the literacy program, and leave solving this Nikki lady's murder to the proper authorities. From what you've told me, it seems entirely possible that our junior senator from Maine might be a murderer. I don't think you want to be the one to expose him."

"I'm surprised to hear you say that," I said.

"Why would that be?"

"It shouldn't matter who the murderer is, Seth. If it was Warren Nebel, senator or no senator, he should be brought to justice."

"That's right," said Seth, "but it doesn't have to be you who does it. Leave it to the police."

I couldn't help but smile. I'd heard this lecture from my dear friend before, but it ran contrary to what I'd already decided, which was to do what I could to help identify Nikki Farlow's murderer.

"Another drink, Jessica?"

I heard Seth, but my mind was on something else.

"Jessica? Another glass of water?" he repeated

"What? Oh, sorry, Seth. I was someplace else."

"Where might that be?"

"I was thinking of my dinner tonight with the lobbyist, Walter Grusin. Something bothers me about our conversation, but I can't pinpoint it."

"It'll come to you, Jessica, probably in the middle of the night. Dreadful thing, that terrorist attack in London. You say your friend, the inspector, is up to his ears in it?"

"Yes. Which reminds me, I want to call him. Mind?"

"Not at all."

I hesitated pulling my cell phone from my purse. I'd developed a true aversion to people who use their portable telephones in public places, including bars and restaurants, and on trains and buses. I checked our immediate vicinity, decided that my voice wouldn't disturb others, and made the call.

It took a few moments before George answered.

"I'm here at the Willard with Seth Hazlitt," I said. "You remember him."

"The good doctor from Cabot Cove. Of course I remember him. Say hello for me."

"I will."

George filled me in on the latest from London, ending

by saying that it looked as though he might have to return home at any moment. I understood, of course, but that didn't ease my disappointment.

"If you're here in the morning, George, perhaps we could have breakfast."

"A splendid idea," he said.

We chose a time to meet in the hotel's dining room, and ended the conversation.

I covered a yawn with my hand and announced it was time for bed. Seth paid the bill, and we went to the lobby. As we waited for an elevator, one of the hotel's assistant managers, who'd personally greeted me when I'd checked in, hurried in our direction.

"Mrs. Fletcher," he said, "I was on my way to your room to deliver this." He handed me a small, sealed envelope. "We just received it. The person who dropped it off said it was urgent that you get it right away."

"Thank you," I said, opening the flap.

"What is it, Jessica?" Seth asked.

"A note from Senator Nebel. His wife attempted suicide tonight."

"Gorry," Seth said, using an all-purpose Maine interjection.

"I've been asked to go to the house."

"For what purpose?" Seth asked.

"I've been spending time with Pat since arriving in Washington. The senator asked me to. She's not well, Seth."

"Anything I can do?" he asked.

"Yes. Will you come with me?"

"Ayuh," he said without hesitation.

We climbed into a waiting taxi, and were on our way to the stately home of Senator and Mrs. Warren Nebel, the site of a lavish dinner party—and a murder.

Chapter Seventeen

The Washington press corps had established a seemingly permanent camp outside the grounds of the Nebel house. A contingent of reporters and technicians sat in director's chairs along the side of the narrow road leading to the property, lights run by generators providing illumination. A uniformed security guard stopped our cab.

"I'm Jessica Fletcher," I announced.

"Yes, ma'am," the guard said, shining the beam of his flashlight on Seth's face.

"This is Dr. Seth Hazlitt," I said.

"No one said anything about him," the guard said. "They told me you'd be coming, but—"

"Please call the house and tell them I have Dr. Hazlitt with me."

The guard did as I asked, and we were told we could pass. I paid the cabdriver, and Seth and I went to the front door. Christine Nebel opened it.

"Hello, Christine," I said. "Nice to see you again. This is Dr. Seth Hazlitt, a friend from home."

"Please come in."

Christine disappeared immediately, but I no longer needed a guide to the house's first floor. I led Seth to the large room at the rear, whose windows overlooked the terrace and river. Jack Nebel was there with press secretary Sandy Teller, attorney Hal Duncan, and a man I didn't recognize. They turned at our entrance.

"Mrs. Fletcher," Teller said, closing the gap between us and extending his hand.

I introduced Seth. The man I didn't know turned out to be the family's Washington physician, Dr. Morris Young, a middle-aged gentleman with a burr haircut, large tortoiseshell glasses, and wearing a blue blazer, gray slacks, and a white shirt open at the neck.

"How is Mrs. Nebel?" I asked.

"She's resting comfortably," Dr. Young answered.

I wanted to ask the details of what had happened, but doubted the doctor would give them to me.

"Is Senator Nebel here?" I asked Teller.

"On his way," he replied. "Could I have a word with you, Mrs. Fletcher?"

"Of course."

We went outside to the terrace.

"I'm sure you'd rather be someplace other than here again," he said.

"Not at all," I said. "Was it you who dropped off the note at my hotel?"

"Yes. The senator asked me to. He didn't want me to do it by phone. Too many potential ears."

"I'd like to know what happened with Mrs. Nebel," I said.

"It's not what people thought at first."

"Meaning?"

"Somebody here panicked and told the senator Pat had attempted suicide. Not true."

"It's not?"

"No. She accidentally took too many sleeping pills."

" 'Accidentally'?"

"That's right."

I read the small smile on his face; he was lying. An attempted suicide by the senator's wife would only add to media speculation about his alleged affair with Nikki Farlow and his possible involvement in her murder. Teller was doing what he was paid to do; put the best possible spin on a bad situation.

"May I see her?" I asked.

"Doc Young says she shouldn't have any visitors."

"Then why am I here?" I asked, not bothering to keep the pique out of my voice.

"It wasn't my idea," Teller said. "The senator told me to deliver his note to the hotel. But since you are here, it gives us the opportunity to talk more about the press and how we'll handle this."

"Mr. Teller," I said firmly, "I have had quite enough of you telling me how *we'll* handle the press. I am not interested in the press or any problems you and the senator might be having with it. I came here as Patricia Nebel's friend, nothing more. Now, if you'll excuse me, I'll go back inside."

"Hey, Mrs. Fletcher, calm down, huh? I'm in a very tenuous position, with Nikki being murdered here at the house, the damn rumors about the senator and her, and now this. Senator Nebel is in a tight race for reelection. This sort of stuff can sink a candidate."

His voice trailed behind as I reentered the house, where Seth was off to one corner with Dr. Young. Duncan, the attorney, had left the room, but the two Nebel children, Jack and Christine, stood near the fireplace. I wasn't sure where to go, but Jack spared me that decision by coming to me.

"It's good of you to be here," he said. "I'm sure Mom will appreciate it."

"How is she?" I asked.

"Okay. Dr. Young wanted her to go to the hospital, but people overrode him."

"What did your mother want to do?" I asked.

"I don't think it mattered to her. She was out of it."

"Who discovered that she'd taken the pills?"

"I did," Jack said. "It was an accident."

"Was it, Jack?"

My challenge caused him to fidget, and to shift from one foot to the other.

"I understand the political ramifications of a tragic suicide attempt," I said, "but it seems to me—and I admit being politically naïve—that some simple honesty would go a long way."

He looked wounded.

"Was it an accident, Jack?" I repeated, "or did your mom try to take her own life?"

"Mom is—"

"I've heard her described as 'delicate' and 'fragile.' I don't believe she's either of those things. At least, that isn't the woman I've always known."

Christine, who'd come up behind Jack, joined us. "I heard you asking about Mom," she said.

"That's right," I said. "If she tried to take her life tonight, she needs more than a stomach pumping. She needs psychiatric care, even if what she did was nothing more than crying out for attention."

Brother and sister looked at each other before Christine spoke. "This isn't a family home," she said. "This is a political campaign headquarters. Nobody cares about what happens to people here, as long as my father's political career is protected." There was unmistakable bitterness, wrapped in sadness, in her quiet voice.

"Christine—" Jack started to say.

"No," Christine said sharply. "Mrs. Fletcher is right. It's time we had some simple honesty."

"Chris is upset," Jack said, trying to explain away his sister's comment.

Christine's eyes welled up, and tears followed. She walked away, passed Seth and Dr. Young, who saw the state she was in, and went through the doors to the terrace. I followed, hoping Teller had left. He had. Christine went to the head of the stairs leading down to the dock, placed her hands on the railing, and sobbed. I placed a hand on her shoulder. "This has been such a difficult time for you and your family," I said. "I'm so sorry."

She turned. Her face was blotchy and wet, but her eyes were angry. "My mother knows about everything," she said.

"What does she know, Christine?"

"About my father and Nikki, about the money, about all of it."

"Christine, don't fall victim to the rumors concerning your father and Nikki Farlow. It may not be what you or your mother think."

"What does *that* mean?"

"I don't believe that your father and Nikki Farlow were anything but professional colleagues."

"How would *you* know?"

"Let's just say that I've learned some things since I've been in Washington that lead me to believe that—to *know* that."

"Because *he* told you?"

"He?"

"My illustrious father, the United States senator. He's a politician. Lying comes easily to him."

I realized I'd created a difficult situation for myself. I'd made a representation to Christine without being willing to back it up with the facts—that Nikki was not a woman who would be interested in an intimate relationship with a member of the opposite sex.

"No," I said, "your father hasn't told me anything. I'm not at liberty to break a confidence, but I think you and your family have been pained by something that isn't there."

She let that noncommittal comment pass and said, "Do you know what she did to Joe?"

"Joe? Your fiancé?"

"That's right."

"Who are you talking about?"

"Nikki. She didn't like Joe from the first time she met him, and poisoned my father about him. She was good at that, poisoning people, setting them against one another. My father was nothing but a pawn in her hands. She ran his life, and our lives, too."

"That's a pretty harsh indictment of her," I said. "I'm not challenging you, but I didn't realize how vehemently you disliked her. Does Joe feel the same way?"

"He hated her. You'll have to excuse me. Joe is picking me up. I want to get out of this place. Thanks for being there for Mom. At least she has one good friend."

I turned to the river, its dark currents catching moonbeams and glittering in the otherwise black night. I'd wanted desperately to share with Christine Nebel why the rumors concerning her father and Nikki Farlow were baseless, and almost had. But I knew that doing so would betray a trust I felt with Nikki's parents, and would address only one of the problems that seemed to be splitting the family apart. Christine's vehement condemnation of her father as a politician was obviously based upon more than whether he was having an affair. She'd branded him a liar—and she'd mentioned money. What had she said? That her mother knew about the affair and the *money*. What was that all about?

I thought back to the dinner party, when Christine's

fiancé, Joe Radisch, had snidely commented that a senator could make a lot more money than his salary. I turned and looked back at the house. I didn't remember how much a United States senator was paid, but it couldn't have been enough to pay for and support what certainly was a mansion and its staff, as well as a home back in Maine.

Seth came through the French doors.

"Pretty fancy place," he commented, turning in a circle to take in the vast expanse of the back of the house.

"Very," I said. "How was your talk with Dr. Young?"

"Nice fella, knows my friend over at NIH. World gets smaller the older I get."

"I've noticed that, too," I said. "What did he have to say about Pat?"

"He didn't say much, but seems she took too many pills."

"Deliberately?"

"Maybe, only the amount she took wouldn't have killed her. Appears to me like a cry for help."

"I feel terrible, Seth. I knew she was upset, but never in my wildest dreams did I think she'd make an attempt on her life."

"Now, Jessica, don't go guiltin' yourself. Most people don't recognize the signs. Sometimes there aren't any."

"Poor thing," I said, "feeling she had to go to that length to get somebody to listen to her."

"The senator stopped by while I was speaking with Dr. Young," Seth said, "came bustling in and disappeared as fast as he arrived. Took off with the lawyer and that Teller fella."

"Have you seen the houseman, Jardine?"

"Ayuh. He asked me and Dr. Young if we wanted a drink." Seth chuckled. "A drink's the last thing I want. Told him some coffee or tea would be nice."

"I'm going inside," I said. "I want to speak with Pat Nebel. After all, that's why we came here."

Jardine was pouring a cup of coffee for Dr. Young when we entered the room. I went to the doctor and asked whether it would be all right for me to see Pat Nebel.

"I understand you're a close friend," he said.

"A friend from back home," I said. "Perhaps it might cheer her up to see me."

He thought for a moment. "Senator Nebel has asked that no one bother her, but in this case . . ." He nodded.

"Thank you; I won't stay long," I said, walking away before he changed his mind.

It occurred to me that while I'd seen much of the house, including her office, I didn't know where the master bedroom was. I turned to find Jardine at my back.

"I'll take you," he said, and led me upstairs, pausing outside a door off a long corridor.

"She's in there," he said in hushed tones.

"Thank you," I whispered. I knocked and slowly opened the door.

Pat was propped up on pillows in a king-size bed. The room was large, thickly carpeted, and expensively furnished in period pieces. Windows dominated the outside wall, offering a view of the river. A single lamp on a night table cast the only light in the room.

She looked up, startled at first, but saw who it was, sat up straight, and waved me to her bedside.

"Hello, Pat," I said.

"Hello to you, Jess," she said, her voice strong. "They dragged you here again, I see."

"They didn't have to drag me," I said. "When I heard that—"

"That I'd done something dumb like overdose on pills. How embarrassing."

"Nothing to be embarrassed about, Pat." I pulled up a small upholstered chair from a dressing table.

"Oh," she said, placing her fingers against her lips. "I forgot. It's supposed to have been an accident."

"That's what they're saying," I said. "An accidental overdose."

"The spin machine in full gear," she said. "Wouldn't look good if Warren's long-suffering wife tried to kill herself. It might give credence to the rumors about Nikki."

"Pat," I said.

"What?"

"Warren wasn't having an affair with Nikki."

She opened her eyes wide and turned to face me.

"Trust me," I said. "They were not having an affair."

"How do you know?"

"It doesn't matter how I know, Pat. What's important is that you believe me."

"But the blackmail." She reached for my hand, and her voice took on urgency. "I heard it, Jess. I heard it with my own ears."

"What exactly did you hear, Pat?"

"I heard Warren discussing it with his attorney, Hal

Duncan. They were trying to figure out how to handle it. I only listened in for a minute or two, but that's why—"

"That's why you thought Warren might have murdered Nikki, to keep her quiet."

"Of course. Doesn't that make sense?"

"Yes, it does. But maybe she was blackmailing Warren about something else, for a different reason." Which I now knew was the case from having read Nikki's letter that Detective Moody had shared with me.

Her expression grew dark, and she turned from me.

"What else could it be?" she asked.

Nikki's letter to the senator hadn't mentioned anything about an affair, but also hadn't been specific about what was behind her threat. Was it money? Joe Radisch's comment at the party, and Christine's mention of it downstairs, coupled with the lavish lifestyle the Nebels were enjoying—at least Warren was enjoying it—made that a distinct possibility.

"Could it have something to do with money?" I asked.

"I don't know what it could be," Pat said.

"If you'd rather not discuss it, I—"

"I really appreciate your being here, Jess, and if you're right about Warren and Nikki, you've done me a very big favor. But I'm suddenly tired, very tired. Would you mind?"

I stood. "Of course," I said, returning my chair to the dressing table. "I'll be downstairs for a while if you need me. Seth Hazlitt came with me tonight."

"Did he? How is he?"

"Just fine. He said to say hello, and that he hopes you're feeling better soon."

"Give him my best."

I backed away from the bed, went to the door, and opened it. Jardine was standing just outside in the hallway, and I had the feeling he'd been listening.

I started toward the stairs, but he stopped me. "May I talk to you?" he asked.

"Of course."

"Not here," he whispered. "I will be at the dock."

"Couldn't we speak here?" I asked in equally hushed tones.

He looked positively panicked. "No, ma'am, not here," he said, looking downstairs over the railing. "I don't want any trouble. The dock. I will go there now."

He ran down the stairs, leaving me on the second floor to ponder what to do. On the one hand, I was determined to not miss this opportunity to hear what he had to say. It undoubtedly concerned Nikki's murder. On the other hand, the thought of going down to the dock at night— the scene of the murder—to meet alone with a man who might well have had something to do with Nikki's death was off-putting.

I went down the stairs and caught up with Seth Hazlitt, who stood by himself staring out the window to the terrace.

"Had your coffee?" I asked.

"Ayuh. How is Mrs. Nebel?"

"She seems fine, a little tired. Feel like some fresh air?"

Once outside, I said, "Seth, I want you to do me a favor."

"What might that be, Jessica?"

"I'm going down those stairs to the dock to meet someone."

"Who?"

"Jardine, the houseman. What I want you to do, Seth, is to stand at the top of the stairs in case I need you. But don't allow yourself to be seen from below. Okay?"

"I do not like this, Jessica Fletcher. Here you go again, puttin' yourself in some kind of dangerous situation."

"I have nothing to worry about as long as I know you're here."

What I didn't say was that I wondered what help Seth could possibly be in the event I actually did need him. He was not in what would pass for good physical shape. Still, just knowing he was there would put my mind somewhat at ease.

"Will you?" I asked.

"Ayuh," he said, obviously not happy about it.

We went to the head of the rickety steps and stopped.

"Stand here," I said, indicating a place where he would not be visible from the dock. "I'll be right back."

As I started down, I looked up and silently thanked an almost full moon for providing a modicum of illumination for my descent. It also occurred to me as I went step by step, my hand firmly gripping the wooden handrail, one foot after the other, that Jardine might not even be there, might have had a change of heart.

I continued until I'd reached the final landing before the dock itself. I squinted to see whether Jardine was there. I didn't see him—but then I did, his silhouette against the pinpoints of light on the crest of ripples in the river.

"Jardine?" I said quietly.

"Yes, ma'am."

We approached each other, stopping a few feet apart.

"What is it you want to tell me?" I asked.

He said nothing in response. He turned and walked quickly away from me, along the dock, past the Aquasport, and to the far end of the dock. I hesitated to follow him into the darkness, but did, stopping a dozen feet away. He turned and looked at me; I moved my hand in the moonlight to indicate I was with him. He nodded—and suddenly disappeared over the side of the dock. For a second I thought he might have fallen into the river. But there was no splash. I slowly went to where he'd been standing. Staying a few feet from where the dock ended, I leaned forward to see where he had gone. There was a lower platform, covered with vines and other shore growth, that jutted out from below the dock. Jardine was on his belly, an arm extended over the edge of the platform. He retrieved something, scrambled to his feet, and walked to me, holding the item he'd pulled from beneath the platform. I couldn't make out what it was until he was directly in front of me. He extended it with both hands, as though presenting me with a sacred sword.

It was a blow poke.

I reached for it, but withdrew my hands.

"I don't understand," I said. "Where did this come from? Why? Did *you* hide it under the deck?"

He walked past me to the foot of the stairs and looked up. I hoped Seth had remained where I'd suggested and couldn't be seen. That was evidently the case, because Jardine returned to where I stood.

"I do not want to be a part of this," he said.

"But you have been," I said. "Did you—"

"I did not kill Miss Nikki," he said. "You must believe me."

"Then why did you end up with this blow poke? It is probably the weapon that killed her."

The words tumbled out of his mouth. "He told me to—"

"Who?"

"Jack. He told me to take the boat and throw this into the river."

"Jack told you to do that?"

"Yes. Yes. He told me."

"But you didn't do it," I said.

"No. Yes, I took the boat but didn't throw this into the river."

"Why?"

"I was afraid. . . . I didn't know what to do. . . . I didn't want trouble. . . . He told me if I didn't do what he said he would send me away. . . . You will help me?"

"Help you? Jardine, the best thing you can do is to give the blow poke to the authorities and tell them everything you know. If Jack killed Nikki, then he will have to face his punishment."

"No, no, they will say I killed her. I know that."

"Jardine, you must listen to me. You have to—"

He thrust the blow poke into my hands and raced up the stairs, leaving me holding the potential murder weapon in my hands.

"Jessica?" Seth called from the top of the stairs. "You all right?"

"Yes. I'm fine. I'm coming up."

I reached the top of the stairs, out of breath and with heavy legs. I leaned against the railing and let out a whoosh of air.

"What's that?" Seth asked, referring to the blow poke and pulling it from my hands.

"Oh, Seth, you shouldn't have," I said. "Your fingerprints are on it now. So are mine."

"Where'd you get this?" he asked.

"It was given to me by the houseman, Jardine."

His expression said he didn't understand.

I took the blow poke from him, using the hem of my light jacket to hold it, and said, "I have to call the police."

Dr. Young had left the house, as had Christine. I went to a telephone on a small rolltop desk, pulled Detective Moody's card from my purse, and dialed his number. I didn't expect to reach him at his office at that hour, but I was wrong. He picked up directly.

"Detective, it's Jessica Fletcher."

"Yes, Mrs. Fletcher. How are you?"

"I have been better," I responded. "Detective, I think you'd better come to Senator Nebel's home right away."

"Oh? What's happened?"

"I believe I have in my hands the weapon that killed Nikki Farlow."

"That blow poke?"

"Yes, sir."

"How did you get it?"

"I'd rather discuss that when you're here. You might bring additional officers with you in case . . ."

"In case what?"

"In case you want to make an arrest."

He said he was leaving immediately.

I hadn't noticed during the tail end of the conversation that attorney Hal Duncan and Nebel's press secretary, Sandy Teller, had entered the room.

"Calling for a taxi?" Duncan asked. He spotted the blow poke and said, "What do you have there?"

"Detective Moody is on his way," I said.

Senator Nebel joined us. "What's going on?" he asked.

I told him about the blow poke, and that the police were coming.

"Where the hell did you get it?" he demanded.

"It might be better if I discuss that with the police," I said firmly.

Seth came to my side.

A minute later sirens were heard, and there was loud knocking at the door. Teller opened it, and Moody and two uniformed officers entered the room. The senator and his attorney had left the room; Teller did, too.

The detective came directly to me.

"Is this it?" he asked, pointing to the blow poke that I'd laid on the desk.

"That's it," I said.

Moody looked at Seth. "Who are you?" he asked.

Seth extended his hand. "I'm Seth Hazlitt, friend of Mrs. Fletcher from back home in Cabot Cove, Maine."

"Seth is a physician," I said.

"Nice meeting you, Doctor," said Moody. To me: "Where's your friend, the Scotland Yard inspector?"

"Busy with the London terrorist attack," I said.

"I came to Washington to be with Mrs. Fletcher," Seth said. "Want to make sure nothing happens to her."

"Oh, Seth," I said, "I don't think—"

Moody pulled a rubber glove from his pocket, picked up the blow poke, and examined it in the light from a lamp on the desk. "Looks like blood, and some hair," he muttered.

"Detective," I said.

He looked at me. "Yes?"

"I think you might want to make sure that Senator Nebel's son, Jack, and the houseman, whose name is Jardine, are still on the premises."

Chapter Eighteen

Moody carried the blow poke to the fireplace and compared its unique handle with handles on the other tools. "Looks like the blow poke we found matches the rest of the set. Unusual design, that's for certain." The officer accompanying Moody had carried in an evidence bag, and Moody handed him the fireplace tool. The officer secured it in the bag, sealed and labeled it. "Take it out to the car and stay with it," Moody ordered.

"I'm afraid you'll find my fingerprints on it," I said, "and Dr. Hazlitt's prints, too. We weren't careful about handling it."

"Important thing is who else's prints are on it. Now, Mrs. Fletcher, what about the son and houseman?"

We were interrupted by the arrival of Senator Nebel. With him was Congresswoman Gail Marshall-Miner, who I assumed had entered the house through a side or rear entrance. Attorney Hal Duncan entered the room right behind them.

"What's this about having found the murder weapon?" Nebel asked.

Moody ignored the senator's question and asked his own: "Is your son at home, sir?"

"My son? Jack? Why do you want to see him?"

"Is he here in the house, sir?" Moody repeated. "And I'd like to speak with the young man who— What's his name?"

"Jardine," I said.

"Right, Jardine," said Moody. "Please get them for me."

"I hate to interrupt your little get-together, Detective," Duncan said, "but are you about to question people about Ms. Farlow's death?" He didn't wait for Moody to respond. "If you are, Detective, I suggest you rethink it. Are you charging someone in her death?"

"Counselor, I—"

"Are you targeting the senator's son or the servant in this matter?"

Moody responded. "I believe, based upon what Mrs. Fletcher has uncovered this evening, that your son, and the male servant— What's his name?"

"Jardine," I supplied again.

"That they might have information bearing upon the murder that took place here," Moody said. "I suggest that if they are in the house, that you bring them down to this room."

"This is absurd," Nebel said. He looked to Duncan for counsel. The attorney nodded, and the two men left the room, leaving us with Congresswoman Marshall-Miner.

"How much can one man take?" she said scornfully. She wore tight jeans, an even tighter teal T-shirt, and sandals. "The rumor about him and Nikki, her murder at his house, that madman trying to shoot him in his office, and now *this*."

I couldn't help myself. "The woman upstairs has had to take a great deal, too," I said.

"Pat?" Marshall-Miner said, a crooked smile on her face. "I'm sure she's doing just fine."

She stomped from the room.

Dr. Young joined us and was introduced to Detective Moody. "I just stopped in to see Mrs. Nebel again," he said. "She's resting comfortably."

"Something wrong with the senator's wife?" Moody asked.

"An accident," Young said. He extended his hand to Seth. "I have to be going. It was a pleasure meeting you, Dr. Hazlitt. Give my best to Tom over at NIH when you see him."

"Ayuh, I'll do that," said Seth.

Young turned to me. "A word, Mrs. Fletcher?"

We went to a far corner of the room. "Your being here and speaking with her was therapeutic," he said. "She mentioned more than once to me how pleased she was that you came."

"It's the least I can do for a friend."

He looked to where Seth and Moody stood, lowered his voice, and said, "When someone attempts to take her own life, Mrs. Fletcher, as feeble an attempt as it might be, it points to an underlying depression that can lead her to try again. The more time you can spend with her over the next few days, the better it will be for her."

"I'll certainly try," I said, "as much as my schedule will allow."

"Good. I don't know how the senator will react, but I intend to send a colleague of mine here tomorrow to evaluate her psychologically. He's a psychologist in whom I have a great deal of faith, very low-key, nonthreatening."

"That seems like a good idea," I said.

"If the senator balks, your support could help."

"Of course," I said. "I'll do what I can."

As he walked away, Detective Moody came to me.

"What sort of accident?" he asked.

"Nothing, really. She'll be fine. About that letter you showed me."

"Yes?"

"Do you have it with you?"

"The copy."

"May I see it again?"

He hesitated, checked that we were not about to be disturbed, pulled the letter from his jacket, and handed it to me. It wasn't a long letter, only two handwritten paragraphs. Its salutation simply said, *Warren*. It was signed, *Nikki*. My second reading of Nikki's words left the same impression as my first exposure had. She was threatening Nebel without being specific. There was no mention of a sexual relationship (not a surprise, considering what I'd learned from her parents of her sexual orientation). Nor did anything she wrote support my speculation that it might have had to do with money. She ended the letter with: *Don't dismiss me, Warren. I can take you down—and will, along with Gail and Barzelouski.*

I refolded the letter and handed it back.

"Why have you allowed me to see this?" I asked.

"Because . . . because I thought you might have some ideas about why she mentions the congressman and congresswoman. I mean, what do they have to do with her blackmailing the senator about the affair they were having? That's what I can't figure out."

I thought for a moment before saying, "I don't think the letter is about the alleged affair they were having, Detective."

" 'Alleged'? Everybody in Washington knows about it."

"Which doesn't mean that everybody in Washington isn't wrong," I said. "That's the problem with rumors like that. If they're repeated enough, they become real. But in this case—"

"Are you saying you know for a fact that there was no affair?"

"Yes," I replied as Seth headed in our direction.

"I'll be damned," Moody said.

"About what?" Seth asked.

"Oh, nothing," Moody said. To me: "How about telling me why you want me to talk to the son and the houseman."

I explained as succinctly as I could how I came in possession of the blow poke, how Jardine led me to it, and that he'd told me he'd been instructed by Jack Nebel to get rid of it.

"Think he was telling the truth?" he asked.

"That he'd taken the blow poke down to the dock? I think that's obvious. Whether Jack Nebel was the one who sent him on that errand remains to be seen."

Hal Duncan strode into the room, fairly pushing Jardine ahead of him.

"Here's who you're looking for," the attorney said.

"Where's the son?" Moody asked.

"Not here," said Duncan.

"Is that so?" Moody said skeptically. "Well, Counselor, I suggest you let the young man know that I intend to talk to him, whether he volunteers or not. I consider him a material witness." He handed Duncan his card. "I'd hate to have to issue a warrant for him, being connected to the senator and all. But if I don't hear from him by noon tomorrow, I'll have to do just that."

Jardine looked at me with pleading eyes. I felt bad for him. Although he'd attempted to dispose of the murder weapon, which constituted obstruction of justice at best, I didn't believe he'd had any part in Nikki Farlow's murder. He'd tried to right an obvious wrong by showing me where the blow poke had been hidden. Had he been guilty, he could have left it there beneath the dock, and no one would have been any wiser. That he had a conscience was obvious.

"Jardine," I said, "this is Detective Moody. I know he has questions for you, and I suggest you cooperate fully with him."

"I didn't do anything," Jardine said, his thin voice breaking. "I didn't kill Ms. Nikki."

"Now, calm down, son," Moody said. "Nobody said

you did. But if what Mrs. Fletcher says is true, you did a dumb thing by hiding what might be the murder weapon."

Moody said to me, "I think it's best if I take him to the precinct and question him there."

"Why did you do this to me?" Jardine asked me, tears in his eyes. "I trusted you."

"Just tell the police the truth, and you'll be fine." I hoped my words reassured him, and that the police would not make me a liar.

Moody called on his radio and the uniformed officer came into the room. "Take this young man out to the car."

When they were gone, Moody said to Seth and me, "I'd better be going. Nice meeting you, Doctor. Your friend here, Mrs. Fletcher, is quite a lady, sharp as a tack. Wouldn't mind having her on my staff."

"Looks like you made quite an impression on him," Seth said as we watched him leave.

"He's a good man," I said, "without an oversize ego to get in the way of his job. But I feel sorry for Jardine."

"Nothin' to feel sorry about, Jessica. He did something wrong. Ready to get out of here?"

"Yes, I think we can go now. Thanks for accompanying me."

"Wouldn't like you to come out here alone at night. With your Scotland Yard friend tied up with terrorists, makes sense for me to stick close."

"And I appreciate that, Seth. Come on. It's been a long day, and I have a feeling tomorrow will be even longer."

Chapter Nineteen

Pleased that the red message light on my phone wasn't flashing when I entered the suite, I undressed, drew my bath, and reveled in the soothing effect of the hot water, embellished with bath oils provided by the hotel. But instead of helping lull me into sleepiness, the bath awakened me. I wrapped myself in a terry-cloth robe, sat on a couch in the living room, and turned on the TV. New information about the terrorist attack in London was included in the newscast, and I wondered what George was doing at that moment. I considered calling him but thought better of it. If he'd managed to catch some sleep, I didn't want to run the risk of disturbing him.

My mind was in high gear. The prime question I grappled with involved the alleged involvement of Jack Nebel. It was natural to speculate that he'd told Jardine to dispose of the blow poke because he'd used it to kill Nikki Farlow.

Or had he decided to get rid of the weapon to shield someone else? Only he could answer that question. I was certain of one thing: Jack had been in the house when Detective Moody was there. It had been easy for Duncan to produce Jardine, whom the family attorney undoubtedly viewed as expendable. Jack Nebel, the son of a powerful U.S. senator, was a different story.

The other question nagging me concerned the letter from Nikki Farlow to Senator Nebel that Detective Moody had shown me. Had Moody received it anonymously? Or did he know the person who'd provided it? And had it been checked for authenticity?

Which led to a third puzzle: What was the significance of Congresswoman Gail Marshall-Miner and Congressman James Barzelouski being mentioned in that letter? My initial thought was that it had to do with something political, perhaps legislation with which they were jointly involved. The lobbyist for Sterling Power, Walter Grusin, had told me that Barzelouski supported the Maine nuclear power plant in the House, and had lent his weight to the literacy program. Surely something as "soft" as a literacy project wouldn't be grist for a scandal. It must have to do with the power plant.

I reflected back on my dinner with Grusin. Something had bothered me about it in retrospect, and I'd mentioned it to Seth. What was it? I still couldn't put my finger on it.

Jardine had admitted to me that the person with whom he'd had an angry exchange on the terrace the night of the party had, in fact, been the son, Jack Nebel.

Because the shoe print had been there when I took a look behind the potted trees, their contentious words had to have taken place *after* Jardine had returned from the boat.

And what of Senator Nebel and his alleged affair with Nikki Farlow? That rumor had developed legs—as goes the saying—and had positioned him as a prime suspect in her murder. Her refusal to acknowledge her homosexuality publicly might have become a contentious issue with the senator. Had he pressured her to come out of that proverbial closet and put a definitive end to the rumor? If she had, it certainly would have wiped that issue from his campaign for a third Senate term. Could he have gotten angry enough at her refusal to kill her? It didn't make sense. He could merely have leaked the information to the press. Perhaps he didn't want his voting public to know there was a homosexual on his staff, afraid the news would turn off a portion of the electorate.

I turned out the lights, slipped between the covers, breathed a contented sigh at the bed's soft comfort, closed my eyes, and fell soundly asleep till the following morning, when I was awakened by the ringing phone.

"Hello?"

"Mrs. Fletcher, this is Greg Farlow, Nikki's father."

I shook the sleep from my head and tried to come up with a reason he'd be calling me. I asked.

"Have you seen the newspaper this morning?"

"No."

"There's a story in it by some reporter named Mumford. Natalie Mumford. Do you know her?"

"We have met."

I didn't have to ask what it was about. Mr. Farlow sounded angry. It had to be about Nikki.

"This reporter," he continued, "has outed Nikki in a national newspaper. My daughter had managed to keep her private life private until you came along. Why did you tell the press?" he demanded.

"Me? Mr. Farlow, I did not tell *anyone* about your daughter. You have my solemn word on that."

"Then how would she get such a story?"

It was bound to happen. The press was relentless when following a hot story. Natalie Mumford had told me she'd come up with information about Nikki through unnamed sources in the Midwest. She'd tried to get me to corroborate it, although why she thought I might be in that position escaped me. I tried to ascertain my culpability in this. Did I have an obligation to recontact Mr. and Mrs. Farlow to inform them that the reporter had developed information about their daughter's sexuality? I hardly thought so. What was important to me at that moment was that I hadn't breached their confidence, not even when doing so would have brought comfort to Pat Nebel. Yes, I'd told her, her daughter, Christine, and Detective Moody that I was certain that no affair existed between Nebel and Nikki. But I'd never stipulated why or how I knew.

Still, I felt for Nikki's parents and their shock at seeing the story that morning.

"Mr. Farlow," I said, "I am very sorry that such a story appeared. Does the reporter"—I was uncomfortable using her name, considering I knew her—"does she identify any sources for her article?"

"All very vague," Greg Farlow responded. "So-called 'reliable sources.' Ha! If it wasn't you, Mrs. Fletcher, I have to assume it was her boss, Senator Nebel."

"Why would you assume that?"

"Get himself off the hook, that's why. Quash the rumor about them having an affair. Politicians! You can't trust a damn one of them."

I really didn't want to get into a debate about the relative trustworthiness of politicians. It was possible Warren Nebel *had* leaked the information.

"I wish I could be more helpful," I said to Greg Farlow, "but I'm afraid I can't. I simply don't know specifically where this reporter got her information. I suggest you call her and ask."

"Fat chance of her being honest with me."

"That may be, but I can't think of anything else to recommend."

We ended the conversation amicably. He apologized for initially accusing me of being the source of the story, and I reiterated that I understood the betrayal they felt, and assured him again that I had not breached his confidence.

I went to the door, opened it, and saw that the newspaper had been left outside. I leafed through but didn't have to go far to find the story—it was on page three, accompanied by a photo of Senator Nebel and Nikki Farlow together at some Washington event earlier in the year. I read the piece with interest. Although "outing" the deceased Nikki Farlow was certainly insensitive, the reporter, Ms. Mumford, had skillfully wrapped it in its political ramification, raising the question of why the senator hadn't come forward with the news that his alleged sexual affair with his top aide was highly unlikely, considering her sexual orientation. Mumford also pointed out that this revelation (from "reliable sources") was likely to take the heat off the senator as a suspect in Nikki's murder. All this aside, it still smacked to me of tabloid journalism wrapped in the paper's lofty image, something I've noticed increasingly lately with so many mainstream newspapers, magazines, and TV news shows. There was one positive thing to come from the article: Pat Nebel, her children, and others who'd been injured by the rumor of an affair now had reason to put it behind them.

I showered and dressed quickly and went downstairs, where Seth was already seated by a window in the Willard Room, reading the morning paper and sipping orange juice, his linen napkin hanging from the front of his collar to protect his shirt.

"Good morning," he said. "Sleep well?"

"Yes, but not long enough. Have you seen the story in the paper this morning about Senator Nebel and Ms. Farlow?"

"Ayuh, I certainly have. And I have a suspicion that you already knew about Ms. Farlow and her . . . her private life."

I nodded. "But I didn't tell anyone. The reporter, or anyone else for that matter."

"Of course you didn't," he said. "You're the most close-mouthed woman I've ever known, and I've known quite a few in my day. Talk to Inspector Sutherland?"

"George? No, I haven't. I'll call him after breakfast. What's on your agenda today?"

"Aside from stickin' close to you, I'm going over to see my friend at NIH. Said he'd show me the latest research he's involved in. Couldn't say no to that."

"I would say not."

"You?" he asked.

"I have to check in with the folks at the Library of Congress. I'm afraid I've almost totally abandoned them, and that's why I came to Washington in the first place. Then I feel compelled to visit with Pat Nebel again. Her doctor asked me to spend as much time with her as possible, and I said I would."

"Then you should. I'll go with you—unless you'd prefer I not."

Knowing Seth as well as I do, I doubted whether he would have taken no for an answer. I gave him my cell phone number before leaving the table and we agreed to touch base later that morning. We said good-bye in front of the hotel and took separate cabs.

I'd consulted my schedule before leaving the suite to meet Seth, and saw that a ninety-minute meeting with the writers associated with the literacy initiative and a group of young children recommended by their teachers would take place at the Library of Congress at ten. I was eager to take part. I'd once been a teacher, and looked forward to sharing my love of books and reading with the youngsters.

"How wonderful to see you," the library's PR woman, Eleanor Atherton, said when I walked into the room. "I thought we'd lost you for good."

"Oh, no," I said with a smile. "You can't get rid of me that easily."

Ms. Atherton took me aside. "What's the latest with the murder?" she asked.

"The murder?"

"At Senator Nebel's home. I read this morning about his aide, Nikki Farlow. That was quite a bombshell."

"I really don't know much more than what's in the papers," I said.

"I just thought that because you were close to the Nebel family, you might—"

"Sorry to disappoint," I said, not wanting to add to Washington's rumor mill. Anyone who thought that Cabot Cove thrived on rumors and gossip needed to spend a few days in our nation's capital.

I was relieved when the children came down the hall, interrupting our conversation. There were thirty of them, boys and girls who looked to be eight or nine years old, led by three teachers.

I joined the other writers— Marsha Jane Grane, Karl von Miller, and Bill Littlefield—in the room where the children were arranged in a semicircle around us. Their bright faces and natural curiosity buoyed my spirits, and I happily participated in the discussion of why reading can become a lifetime companion, a continuing source of pleasure and knowledge. The children's questions and comments were delightful, their individual personalities shining through, some funny without meaning to be, others extremely serious, all a delight with whom to spend time. Karl von Miller proved to be their favorite, no surprise considering that he wrote books for young readers. He was a superb storyteller who held the children in his spell—held me in his spell, too. Marsha Jane Grane seemed uncomfortable dealing with youngsters, many of her answers to their questions above their heads. But she was obviously trying hard to fit in, for which I gave her credit.

When Ms. Atherton shifted the subject to murder mysteries, there were lots of oohs and aahs from the children. I asked them to create a mystery story on the spot, and their myriad suggestions were wonderful, leaving me to wonder whether I would eventually read a novel of that genre written by one of them.

The hour and a half flew by. As we were getting ready to end the session, a TV camera crew and reporter arrived to do a piece on the program. We extended the time together for their benefit, engaging the students in more discussion for the camera. Once the children were taken from the room, the reporter asked to interview Ms. Atherton and me. I was hesitant; I didn't want the reporter to ask questions about anything to do with Senator Nebel and Nikki Farlow. But I agreed, and she stuck to the subject of literacy and the project for which I'd come to Washington. With the camera and microphone off, she did ask me whether Mrs. Nebel would be making any appearances in connection with the program she'd initiated, with her husband's support.

"I really don't know," I said.

"I was wondering," she said, "because of the incident last night. We've heard that she accidentally overdosed on pills."

There evidently was no such thing as a secret in Washington, but I was not about to confirm her information. "Sorry, I can't help you there," I said.

I promised the other writers in the group that I would catch up with them later, and went to Atherton's office, from which I called George Sutherland's cell phone.

"Sutherland here," he answered.

"It's Jessica."

"Ah, my dear, I'm so sorry to have abandoned you. How are you?"

"I understand, George. I'm fine. You?"

"Things are finally under control, although I'm afraid I will have to head off in a day or two. I was hoping we could grab some time together before that. Up for dinner?"

"Are you sure you can break away?" I asked.

"At the moment all is quiet. No one has claimed credit for the attack in London, and there hasn't been much progress in rooting out the devils. We'll be launching a major investigation when I get back. That should tie me up for months. About dinner?"

"Yes, of course. I'm heading for the Nebels' to spend some time with Pat. She overdosed on pills last night."

"Good Lord. Is she all right?"

"Fortunately, yes, but I promised her doctor I'd stop in and see her. Tell you what. I'll call you at the end of the day, say five-ish, and we'll make plans. Sound good?"

"Yes, it does."

I remembered that Seth was in town and would want to spend time with me, too. As much as I wanted to, I was torn. There was no telling how long it would be before I again saw George. I could see Seth virtually every day back home in Cabot Cove. Was I rationalizing? Of course I was. I decided to play it by ear later, and didn't mention to George that it might end up being a threesome.

I tried Seth's cell number but reached only his voice mail; he'd evidently forgotten to turn on his phone. I'd go to the Nebel house alone and try him again.

As I rode in the back of a taxi to McLean, it occurred to me that the literacy programs were coming to an end, and with them my time in Washington. If I wanted to get to the bottom of Nikki Farlow's murder, I'd have to move fast. Otherwise I'd go home without the answer, which would be frustrating. I'm one of those people who hate unresolved questions. Once I become involved in something, I need answers. Call it impatience. Call it nosiness. Call it a need for instant gratification. No matter what it represents it's part of my basic nature, and I accept it.

I was surprised when Senator Nebel answered my knock.

"Jessica," he said. "I didn't know you were coming."

I told him why.

"You read the paper this morning," he said flatly.

"Yes. I assume you knew all along about Ms. Farlow's sexual orientation."

"Of course I did. And I hasten to say that I respected her wish that it not become public knowledge, even though keeping her secret, even after her death, has caused me a number of problems."

"That's admirable," I said. "But it must have been

tempting to do just that, make it public to put an end to the rumor about you and her."

"Of course it was. I consider myself an honorable man. I respect those who work for me, and that includes keeping their confidences."

I wasn't sure I should ask about the letter, but fell back on my decision to be direct in the interest of time.

"I may be out of line, Senator, in asking this," I said, "but since I've been drawn into this situation, I feel justified."

His smile was fatherly as he placed a hand on my shoulder and said, "Jessica, you can ask me anything you want."

I didn't hesitate: "Was Nikki blackmailing you? She was accusing you of something. Why? What was it?"

My question wiped the smile from his handsome face. His expression turned to stone. He removed his hand from my shoulder and said in a slow, measured voice, "I resent that question, Jessica. I resent it mightily. Perhaps you should leave."

"I'm here to see Pat," I countered. "Dr. Young asked me to."

"Be that as it may, I remind you that you're here in Washington because of me and the literacy program. You're a writer, not a cop or a politician. I suggest you remember that."

"Oh, I'm well aware of why I'm here, Senator, and of who I am. But now that any allegation of an affair between you and Ms. Farlow seems moot, the question of why she would write you a threatening letter looms large."

"Letter?"

"Yes. I've seen a copy of it."

"Who gave it to you? I'll—"

"It doesn't matter who showed me the letter," I said. "What is important is that it exists. Why did Nikki write that letter? Look, Senator, I agree that such a letter is highly personal; however, it might have some significance in Nikki's murder. I'm sure you're as anxious as I am to see her killer brought to justice."

My little speech gave him time to compose himself. The smile reappeared, and his posture relaxed. "That letter," he said, "had to do with politics, pure and simple, Jessica. It has absolutely nothing to do with Nikki's tragic demise. You can take that to the bank! Now, let me ask *you* something."

"All right."

"Who showed you that letter?"

"I really can't betray that confidence," I said.

"Well," he said, "I'll find out who leaked it, and when I do, that someone will be very sorry."

I didn't say anything.

"Was it someone from my staff?" he asked.

"Senator Nebel, I cannot—"

"Excuse me," he said smoothly. He smiled, but his eyes were rock-hard. "I'm afraid I have to get back to my office. Why don't I give you a ride into town?"

"Thank you," I said, "but I came here to spend time with Pat."

"She's resting. She can't see anyone now."

"But—"

"Sorry, Jessica. Looks like you made the trip for nothing."

I considered arguing the point but thought better of it, and accepted his offer.

It was obvious during our trip that Nebel wasn't about to discuss anything having to do with the letter or Nikki Farlow's murder. He drove fast, too fast for my taste, and launched into a monologue on the pressures of being a United States senator, particularly when dealing with a contentious subject like the power plant in Cabot Cove. I was content to listen; I knew any further attempts to gain information from him about other things would prove futile. I told him when we entered the city—the District, as it's commonly known—that there wasn't any need to take me to the hotel. But he insisted, and dropped me off at its front door. He reached across me and opened my door, smiling as he did. "Jessica," he said, "I just want you to know how much Pat and I appreciate what you're doing for the literacy drive."

"Thank you," I said. "And thank you for the ride."

I got out of the car. He closed the door, gave me a flip of the hand, and drove off.

"Good afternoon," the Willard's doorman on duty said to me as he held open the door.

That remains to be seen, I thought.

I smiled and returned his greeting.

Chapter Twenty

Although I'd been brimming with energy since being awakened that morning by Nikki's father, a wave of fatigue swept over me the minute I walked into my suite. I sat on the bed, kicked off my shoes, and made a decision. I needed some time for myself, and pledged to find it then and there. It would take a fire in the hotel, or an act of Congress, to drag me from the lovely suite in which I'd spent far too little time.

I changed into comfortable clothes, closed the drapes, retrieved a paperback book I'd bought at the airport from my bag, and curled up on the couch. Before starting to read, I called George on his cell.

"Hello, Jessica," he said happily. "Where are you?"

"In my hotel suite. I decided I need some time alone to recharge the batteries—which, I might add, seem suddenly to have discharged."

"Glad to hear that. Not about your batteries, but your

decision to get off the treadmill. Will you feel well enough for dinner?"

"Of course. A few hours of solitude, aided by a nap, will do wonders. Seven? Is that good for you?"

"That's fine. A colleague here has recommended a restaurant she says is splendid. I wrote it down somewhere. Ah, yes, here it is. Citronelle. 'French with a California influence' is the way she describes it."

"Sounds lovely."

"Good. I'll make a reservation for seven. Meet you there?" He gave me the address and phone number.

"I'll be fresh as a daisy and on time," I said.

I fell asleep after only a few pages of the book, which wasn't an editorial comment on the author. My eyes had become so heavy that I simply couldn't hold them open any longer. My final thought before succumbing was whether I should leave a wake-up call. But I couldn't stay awake long enough to do even that.

As it turned out, I didn't have to. The phone rang a half hour after I'd dozed off. It sounded frightfully loud, and jerked me awake. I shook my head and tried to blink away the sleep as I stumbled across the room and picked up the phone.

"Mrs. Fletcher?"

"Yes."

"It's Richard Carraway. Senator Nebel's aide."

"Yes. Hello. I'm sorry if I sound groggy but your call woke me."

"Sorry. Didn't mean to do that. Mrs. Fletcher, I have to talk with you."

"All right. I think I'm sufficiently awake now to have a rational conversation."

"No, no, in person. I must see you in person."

"I'm afraid I'm really not up to that, Mr. Carraway."

"Please."

It sounded as though his voice had cracked. Was he attempting to hold back tears?

"Look, Mrs. Fletcher, it's about Nikki's murder. I know something about that."

"Oh? Then I suggest you immediately call Detective Moody with the Fairfax County police."

"I can't do that. And . . ."

"And?"

"I'm not sure I'll be alive long enough to tell anyone. Please meet with me and I'll tell you everything. You seem to be the only one involved who doesn't have your own agenda, except maybe to get to the bottom of Nikki's murder. I'm involved in a conference on a bill the House passed and the Senate is trying to amend. I can be out of here by six."

"Six! I have a dinner engagement at seven. Wait a minute. What did you mean when you said you might not live long enough? Are you ill?"

"I'm afraid I'm going to end up like Nikki."

I was momentarily speechless.

Carraway barreled ahead. "I promise I won't make you late, Mrs. Fletcher. Please. I don't want to beg, but—"

"All right. I'll meet you at six. Would you like to come to the hotel?"

"No. Too public. Meet me at the National Cathedral."

"The National Cathedral? Mr. Carraway, I—"

"It's quiet there and we can be alone. I'll meet you in the Bishop's Garden, in the Rose Garden area. It's next to the cathedral. Take a taxi. I'll reimburse you."

"Mr. Carraway, I am perfectly capable of paying for my own cab ride. I'll see you at six."

I almost had a change of mind, but he hung up before I could say more. So much for my tranquil respite. I had a feeling I'd been neatly maneuvered. He'd never have gotten around me so easily if I hadn't been groggy.

There was still some time to kill before having to leave for my meeting with Carraway, and I considered resuming my nap. But there was no way I would fall asleep again, and even if I managed to drift off, I was afraid I'd awaken even more tired. I usually travel with an exercise videotape, and this trip was no exception. I put it in the VCR and spent the next half hour limbering up and getting my blood flowing with aerobics. That helped the rejuvenation effort. I took a quick shower and dressed in an outfit appropriate to having dinner later with George at a fancy French restaurant. With still some time before having to leave, I opened one of the guidebooks I'd carried to Washington and read about the National Cathedral, also known as the Cathedral Church of St. Peter and Paul, or Washington Cathedral. As much as I wasn't looking forward to meeting with Richard Carraway, I experienced two parallel feelings: I was intensely curious about what he had to offer regarding the murder on Nikki Farlow, and I was looking forward to seeing the cathedral, one of too many of Washington's imposing landmarks that I'd not gotten around to visiting on previous trips. If it weren't for Carraway's call, I wouldn't have seen it on this trip, either.

I was preparing to leave when I remembered that I'd never gotten hold of Seth. This time my call to his cell was answered.

"I tried you earlier," I said, "but you didn't have your phone on."

"I know. Plumb forgot. So how did your day go, Jessica?"

"Eventful, Seth. I'll fill you in when I see you."

"I was plannin' on dinner tonight. I'll be heading back to Cabot Cove day after tomorrow."

"So will I."

I was thinking about my dinner plans with George. Should I invite Seth? Although I looked forward to time alone with George, I couldn't exclude one of my dearest friends in this world; nor could I lie to him about my plans.

"George Sutherland called and suggested dinner," I said, "and I accepted. Why don't you join us? It would be nice having the three of us together."

There was silence on his end. Then he said, "Where were you plannin' on going? Some fancy French place?"

"As a matter of fact, that's exactly what we planned. George says it's highly recommended. It's called Citronelle. How did he describe it? Sort of French with a California influence."

Another silence. Dr. Seth Hazlitt is the quintessential meat-and-potatoes man, despite how that approach does little for cholesterol levels, to say nothing of calories.

"Well?" I said.

"Ayuh," he said.

"Wonderful." I gave him the address of the restaurant, and we agreed to meet there at seven.

I went to the lobby, through the doors, and climbed into a taxi whistled to the entrance by the doorman.

"Where to?" the driver asked.

"The National Cathedral," I replied. "On Wisconsin and Massachusetts avenues."

"I know where it is," he said gruffly, slipping the cab into gear and making a noisy getaway from the curb, followed by a plume of noxious smoke. It occurred to me, as it often does when traveling by cab in American cities, that once you've experienced London's wonderful, comfortable, well-maintained taxis driven by polite, well-trained professionals, you can never be truly pleased.

After we'd been driving for a few minutes, I happened to look back through the rear window and noticed a black Mercedes behind us. I didn't give it another thought until we'd turned onto the access road to the cathedral, and I saw that the Mercedes, which had obviously been trailing us the entire way, had also pulled on to the access road. I'm certainly not a paranoid person, but I couldn't help but wonder if Carraway was having me followed.

The cabdriver came to a stop in front of the cathedral, the spire of which soared majestically into the sky. I paid him what he said I owed (I much prefer meters to Washington's system of zones, having to know, or guess, how many zones you'd traversed), got out, and approached the cathedral. Its size and splendor were awe-inspiring, as was its stated mission, as defined by Congress in 1893: "a national house of prayer for all people." How wonderful to have a national place of prayer regardless of one's religion of birth or beliefs.

I was early; it was five-thirty. The driver had driven fast, too fast. Oh, well, I thought, I would have time to spend a few minutes inside the cathedral itself, where I could ask directions to the gardens. Before entering, I looked back and saw that the Mercedes had come closer, but had stopped a hundred yards from where I stood. For a moment I considered approaching the driver and asking what he was doing. But I discarded that notion. It was probably nothing more than a coincidence, and I didn't want to look foolish.

I stepped into the nave, a tenth of a mile long from rear to altar, and was immediately overwhelmed by the interior splendor. Huge stained-glass windows high above caught the day's fading sunlight and cast multicolored shafts of light, creating a kaleidoscope of red and blue, yellow and purple.

There was total silence. I narrowed my eyes to survey the pews that stretched from where I stood to the imposing altar. I seemed to be the only person there, alone in this monument to man's creativity and spirit, and to our need to build tributes to the gods, no matter who they might be. Outside, it was hot and humid. Here, surrounded by countless tons of Indiana limestone, it was refreshingly cool. I drew a breath; the lingering scent of incense filled my nostrils.

I glanced at the entrance to see if anyone had followed

me inside. Seeing no one, I walked to the south transept and lingered in the War Memorial Chapel, dedicated to the men and women who'd lost their lives in defense of the country. It was one of nine chapels in the cathedral, and was dominated by a huge needlepoint tapestry called the *Tree of Life,* on which the seals of the fifty states were rendered in petit point.

I moved from there to the Children's Chapel, where everything was child-size—scaled-down seats, low altar, and miniature needlepoint kneeling pads depicting family pets and wild beasts, including Noah's Ark's passenger list. Even the organ was small. The chapel celebrated the worth and dignity of children and four-legged animals, the most vulnerable and dependent of all creatures. A statue of the Christ child stood near the entrance, its arms open wide in welcome. I approached the statue and saw that the bronze fingers on one outstretched hand were shiny, in contract to the rest of the sculptured figure that had burnished with age. How many visiting children had grabbed hold of those bronze fingers and kept them bright? I wondered.

I was so at peace with myself and the world that I'd forgotten about the Mercedes and had even neglected to keep tabs on the time. It was close to six, when I was to meet Carraway. I walked quickly out a side door. It was a fortuitous choice of exits. A sign across the road indicated the way to the Bishop's Garden.

I crossed the road and followed signs that led through the Norman Arch and the gardens beyond. It was heading toward darkness. The trees, coupled with low, black clouds that had rolled in from the west, had turned day into almost night. I followed a winding path until reaching the Rose Garden, filled with floribundas and hybrid tea roses of varying hues. Carraway stood beneath an aging pear tree.

"Hello," I said.

His nervousness was palpable. His head was in constant motion, looking left and right, and past me as though to see whether I'd come alone.

"Hello," he managed. "Thank you for coming. No one is with you, is there?"

"No," I said. "No one is with me. I suggest you get right to the point, Mr. Carraway. As I said, I have a dinner engagement at seven."

"I know, I know," he said, moving to a small bench to his right and plopping down on it. I debated joining him but decided to continue standing.

"You said you feared for your life," I said, hoping to jump-start the conversation. "What did you mean?"

He pulled a handkerchief from his suit jacket pocket and wiped his brow and the back of his neck. Then, as though he'd suddenly heard my question, he jerked and said, "Sit down, please, Mrs. Fletcher."

I reluctantly did. I faced him and waited for an answer.

"I know too much," he said. "Like Nikki."

"Know what?" I asked.

"Why she was murdered."

He got to his feet and surveyed the garden again for signs of intruders.

"I'm listening," I said. "Why was she murdered?"

"To shut her up, that's why. They'll do the same to me."

"What did she know that would cause someone to want her dead?" I asked.

He drew a series of deep breaths, rejoined me on the bench, and looked into my eyes beseechingly. "I come here a lot," he said, the subject totally changed. "Sometimes I get so mad I want to kill somebody, and I come here and it relaxes me, makes those feelings go away."

"That's certainly better than acting out your angry feelings," I said. "But—"

"Like when Nebel hired Nikki and demoted me. I wanted to kill him *and* her."

"You were saying something about what Nikki knew that got her killed, Mr. Carraway."

"Please call me Richard."

"All right, Richard. Now, what did Nikki know? Nothing will be accomplished if you keep circumventing the issue."

Another series of deep breaths before saying, "She knew about the payoffs."

"Payoffs? To whom?"

"Lots of people. Senators. Congressmen."

"Senator Nebel?"

Panic crossed his round face. "Yeah, the senator has been on the take big-time."

I paused to put my thoughts together before asking, "And Nikki was blackmailing him about the money?"

He shook his head. "I never liked Nikki, Mrs. Fletcher. I already told you that. But I'll say one thing about her:

She was a straight shooter, straight as an arrow when it came to government and money and the like. When she took over my job, she was up to her neck in legislative matters, including the Sterling Power plant in Maine. But when Nebel got wind she'd discovered the payoffs, he shifted her to more administrative duties and handed me back the legislation. But she wouldn't let go. She kept digging until she came up with proof of the payoffs. That's when she wrote that letter to him."

"The threatening letter," I said.

"You know about that?"

"Yes. Did you provide that letter to Detective Moody?"

He shrugged. "I thought maybe it would help him in his investigation."

"I'm sure it has," I said. "The letter refers to Congressman Barzelouski. It also talks about Gail. I assume that's Congresswoman Marshall-Miner."

"They've been on the take, too."

"You mentioned Sterling Power. Is Mr. Grusin the source of illegal payments to the senator and others?"

He guffawed. "Who else?" he replied. "He's been funneling money—big money—to the senator and the others."

"What constitutes big money?" I asked.

I detected the hint of a smile on his otherwise sour face. "A million to the senator."

My gasp was involuntary. "A million dollars?" I said.

"That's right."

"For his vote on the power plant?"

"Yes."

"I see why you might be concerned about your safety. Let me ask you something. Were you aware that Nikki wasn't really having an affair with Senator Nebel?"

"Yeah. 'Cause she was gay, right?"

I sighed and nodded. "Yes."

"I knew that, but not right away."

"Why didn't the senator make it public in some way to quash the rumors of the affair? Was it because he respected Nikki's wish to have her sexual orientation kept private?"

Another small smile from him as he replied, "The senator's only interested in his own secrets, not anyone else's."

"But he could have exploded that rumor of an affair, and he didn't."

"It was better to let that rumor fly than one about Gail Marshall-Miner."

This time the smile was on my lips. I'd suspected there was something going on between Nebel and the congresswoman beyond their political and professional relationship in Congress. Grusin had hinted at it, and now Carraway had confirmed it. I also suspected that Senator Nebel's reason for not leaking Nikki's sexual orientation was something other than altruistic. Keeping the rumor going about him and Nikki might have served to keep his wife from suspecting he was having an affair with Gail. He could tell her with a straight face that there was nothing between him and Nikki—because there wasn't.

I glanced at my watch. It was twenty of seven.

"Richard, "I said, "I appreciate your telling me these things. The question is, why me?"

"I had to unload on somebody," he responded. "Oh, I've told the story a couple of times to my priest. I knew he'd have to keep it confidential between us. But I wanted to make someone else aware, someone like you. Maybe if enough people know, there won't be any need to kill me."

I stood. "I must go," I said. "I'm afraid I'm already running late."

"I'll drive you to your appointment," he said.

"Thank you. I appreciate that."

We walked from the Bishop's Garden to where he'd parked his car. As we approached it, I saw a man exit quickly from the cathedral through its main entrance and fairly run to his car, the black Mercedes. He got in, started the engine, and drove off.

"Strange," I said.

"What is?" Carraway asked.

"That man who came out of the cathedral. I could swear it was Jack Nebel."

"Why would he be here?" Carraway asked.

"I have no idea," I said. "And I'm probably wrong. I only had a fleeting glimpse of him." Still . . .

It wasn't until we'd reached the heart of Georgetown and the Latham Hotel, in which Citronelle was located, that I saw the Mercedes again. It drove past us as Carraway pulled up in front of the hotel. Once more I had only a fleeting glance at the driver, but this time I was certain who I'd seen. It *was* Jack Nebel.

I thanked Carraway for the ride.

"No problem," he said. "What are you going to do now? You know? With what I told you?"

"That's all that's been on my mind on the way here," I said. "Richard, do you think you could arrange for certain people to meet us at the senator's house tomorrow?"

"What people?"

"Congresswoman Marshall-Miner and Congressman Barzelouski?"

"I can try."

"That's all I can ask."

"What about the senator?"

"I believe I can convince him to be there," I said. "And his family, too. What about Walter Grusin? Can you contact him?"

"Sure. I don't know if he'll come, but I'll give it a shot. What time?"

"Let's say one o'clock."

"Okay, Mrs. Fletcher."

"Good."

"Mrs. Fletcher?"

"Yes?"

"Thanks for listening. I think that for maybe the first time in my life, I picked the right person to confide in."

"That's flattering. Safe home, Richard. With a little luck, this will all be resolved tomorrow."

Seth was waiting at the bar when I entered the restaurant. I didn't see George. It was seven-fifteen. I'd never known George to be late.

Seth read my mind as I approached. "Haven't seen your Scotland Yard friend," he said.

"He must have gotten tied up with the terrorist investigation," I said. "I'm surprised he hasn't called. He has my cell number."

"What held *you* up?" Seth asked.

"It's a long story. I'll tell you over dinner."

"I suggest we take the table, unless you'd like a drink here at the bar."

"No drink for me," I said, "but let me try to reach George from here. I wouldn't want to disturb other diners by making a call."

I reached his voice mail.

We went to the table that had been reserved in the name of George Sutherland, and settled in for a lovely dinner, three courses price-fixed at seventy-five dollars a person. But I'm afraid I wasn't the most receptive of dinner companions. I kept thinking of what Carraway had told me, and of Jack Nebel and why he would have been following me. And, as time passed, I grew increasingly worried about George. After our first course, I excused myself, went to the ladies' room, and tried George again. No luck.

Over our entrée—lobster medallions with garnishes of sliced artichoke bottoms and Jerusalem artichokes, nestled in a fried nest of finely shredded potatoes—which the jaded Dr. Hazlitt pronounced "*Magnifique!*"—I recounted for him what Carraway had told me at the cathedral. He listened with rapt attention, interrupting only occasionally to ask me to clarify a point. When I was finished, he said, "Looks like we've got ourselves a crooked senator from Maine, Jessica. What do you intend to do with what you've learned?"

"I don't know," I replied honestly, although a plan had begun to formulate in my mind.

Our third and final course was about to be served when a manager came to the table. "Mrs. Fletcher?" he said.

"Yes."

"You have a call from Inspector Sutherland."

"Wonderful," I said. I excused myself from Seth and followed the manager to a phone.

"George, are you all right?" I asked immediately.

"I've been better, love," he said.

"What's wrong? Another terrorist attack?"

"In a manner of speaking. One of Washington's terrorists mugged me."

"*What?*"

"I was on my way to meet you when it happened. Three of them, actually. Young randies. That's Scottish for thugs. Hooligans."

"Good heavens! Are you hurt badly?"

"Got banged in the head pretty good. The doctors here at the hospital won't let me leave. Protocol, they say, with my kind of head injury."

"What hospital?"

"At your George Washington University."

"Seth and I will be there in twenty minutes," I said.

"No, no, Jessica, please, no. I look a bit of a mess, and my ego is sufficient that I'd prefer you to see me when I've had a bit of time to return to my handsome, dashing self."

I started to protest, but he insisted.

"Get yourself a good night's sleep and give me a ring

in the morning. Sorry I couldn't call earlier. The doctors were sewing me up. Talk with you tomorrow?"

"All right," I said reluctantly. "You're sure you're going to be all right?"

"I'll be tip-top, I assure you. The doctors assure me of that, too. Best to your doctor friend. Tell him I'm in good hands."

"I will."

"This is a dangerous city," Seth said after I'd returned to the table and told him what had happened.

"No more so than most cities," I said. "Could have happened anywhere."

"Ayuh, but it happened here. Want me to go over and check on him, make sure the staff is up to snuff?"

"He doesn't want any visitors," I said. "Let's enjoy what's left of this wonderful dinner and get back to the hotel."

On the way out, Seth cornered the manager who'd informed me of George's call and said, "Name's Dr. Seth Hazlitt, from Cabot Cove, Maine. Got a question for you."

"Yes, sir?"

"Tried cooking lobster medallions myself a few times, but they always ended up tough. What's your secret?"

"Chef Richard cooks the medallions in a two-hundred-and-seventy-five-degree oven for approximately twenty-five minutes," he said. "It mustn't be too hot or the lobster meat turns rubbery."

"Much obliged," Seth said, overtly pleased that he'd learned a trade secret from a master chef.

I looked for the Mercedes when we came out of the

hotel but it was nowhere in sight. We took a taxi to the Willard and parted in its opulent lobby. I went to my suite and got ready for bed, my head swirling with all that had happened that evening. I sat up for a few hours scribbling notes of the conclusions to which I'd come over the course of the evening, forcing myself to concentrate and not let my thoughts wander to George and his injuries. By the time I climbed into bed, everything had jelled. Barring any unforeseen events, I felt confident I had the answer to Nikki Farlow's murder.

And I intended to reveal that answer the next day.

Chapter Twenty-one

I was up early, long before my wake-up call. (I'm never sure how to set those silly little clock radios in hotels and always leave a wake-up call as insurance.) I'd told Seth when we parted last evening that I intended to have breakfast in my room because I had a number of calls to make, but I asked if he would agree to accompany me to Senator Nebel's. We set a time to meet.

My first call was to Nebel's office in the Dirksen Building. Carraway answered.

"You're there early," I said.

"I always am," he said. He lowered his voice: "I called Grusin and Marshall-Miner at home last evening. They'll be there."

"What did you tell them?"

"I lied, which I figured was okay. I told them the senator wanted them there to discuss the Sterling Power legislation."

"I'm glad you filled me in," I said. "I'll know what to expect when I call the senator. What about Congressman Barzelouski?"

"He was out all evening, but I left a message on his machine."

"Good. I'll see you later."

My next call was to the Nebel house, where Jack answered.

"Hope I'm not waking anyone," I said cheerfully.

"We're up," he said, "and I'm glad you called. I understand you told that detective that I gave the blow poke to Jardine."

"Not true," I said. "All I did was pass along to Detective Moody what Jardine had told me."

"Well, I don't think you had any right to do that, Mrs. Fletcher."

"Did you have the right to follow me last night when I went to the National Cathedral?" I countered.

"What are you talking about?"

"I'm afraid you wouldn't make a very good private investigator. I was well aware it was you driving the black Mercedes last evening."

"Look, Mrs. Fletcher, things aren't the way they might appear to be. The whole thing with the blow poke, and wanting to see where you went last night were—"

"Jack, why don't we discuss all this when I come to the house later today?"

"You're coming to see Mom?"

"Yes, and I'd like you to be there."

"What is this?" he asked.

Instead of answering, I asked whether his sister was at the house. When he told me she was, I asked to speak with her.

"Tell me what's going on," he demanded.

"I'd really prefer to talk with you in person," I replied. "May I speak with Christine now, please?"

Christine came on the line.

"I'm planning to be at the house about one," I said. "Can you be there?"

"I suppose so."

"I'd really like your fiancé, Mr. Radisch, to be there, too."

"Joe is coming by to take me to lunch."

"Perfect," I said. "Perhaps you can delay your meal for a little while."

"Does this have to do with Nikki's murder?" she asked.

"Let's discuss the reason for it when I'm there. Is Mrs. Martinez available?"

"Carmela? Yes. She's in the kitchen."

"Would you put her on?"

I introduced myself to the cook and told her of my plans to gather a number of people at the house that day. I didn't want her taken by surprise if her employers asked her to furnish refreshments. She was pleasant and helpful.

"Do you want me to serve lunch?"

"I don't think that's necessary," I said, "and I don't want to impose on either you or the Nebels." What I didn't say was that the subject of the gathering was likely to spoil the guests' appetites. I asked if she knew whether or not the senator was at home and she said he wasn't, that he'd left very early for his office.

By the time I made my second call to Nebel's office, his secretary was there and answered. She put me through to an overtly irate senator.

"What's this about a meeting at my house today?" he growled.

"That's why I'm calling," I said, maintaining a lilt in my voice. "I wanted to thank you and your family for all your hospitality since I've been here, to me and to my friends Dr. Hazlitt and Inspector Sutherland."

He wasn't buying it.

"Cut the crap, Jessica. I've already heard from Walt Grusin and Congresswoman Marshall-Miner. They said that Carraway told them it was to discuss the Cabot Cove power plant. What are you up to?"

"Is Mr. Carraway there?" I asked.

"No, dammit. He left a note saying he was out on meetings all morning and would see me at the house. Now, Jessica Fletcher, what is going on?"

It was obvious I wasn't going to be able to finesse the situation any longer.

"Senator Nebel," I said, "there's an unsolved murder of your top aide to be resolved. It happened at your house, at a party you hosted. I believe I know who murdered Nikki Farlow, and I think you'll want to know as well."

"I don't see where anyone you've invited—to *my* house, I might add—has anything to do with Nikki's death. This is a joke." His laugh was dismissive. "You don't know what you're talking about," he said. "None of my people had anything to do with it, and you can take the word of a United States senator on that."

I said nothing.

Now his laugh was forced, conciliatory. "I will say this, Jessica. You have a very fertile imagination. But I suppose that's to be expected of a successful mystery writer."

"Senator," I said, "why don't you simply come to your house at one and hear me out? I'm sure you'll find what I have to say enlightening."

"All right," he grumbled, "but leave Pat out of it."

"Even if she wants to attend?"

"She's not well."

I didn't say what I was thinking, that Patricia Nebel was probably a lot less "sick" than some of those around her. Still, I wouldn't impose on her. I would simply make her aware of our presence and let her decide whether she wished to come downstairs or not.

Nebel abruptly ended the conversation, and I placed a call to Detective Moody's office at the Fairfax County Police Department. They paged him and he eventually came on the line. I told him about the gathering I'd planned, and said I needed him to be there, preferably with a couple of uniformed officers outside. He pumped me for information, but I was steadfast in my determination to save my conclusions until we met. His final comment before we ended the call was, "Why do I have the feeling I'm a character in one of your murder mysteries, Mrs. Fletcher?"

I laughed and said, "I assure you this isn't fiction, Detective. You'll be there?"

"Wouldn't miss it," he said, his words punctuated with a low, rumbling laugh.

All the calls on my list completed, I looked up the number for the George Washington University Hospital and was connected with George's room.

"Good morning, love," he said.

"Good morning to you. How are you feeling today?"

"Not bad aside from a whopping headache. But I've got good news. If I pass some tests they insist upon giving me later, I'll be able to leave by day's end."

"I'm so pleased to hear that," I said. "Maybe we'll finally find some time together."

"No maybes about it, Jessica. We shall. My recovery won't be complete without it. What is on *your* agenda?"

"I'm attending a meeting at Senator Nebel's house."

"Oh? Sort of a farewell gathering?"

"You might say that. I really must run, George. Be a good patient, pass your tests, and I'll be in touch later this afternoon."

I spent the next forty-five minutes on the phone with people involved with the literacy program, offering my apologies for my lack of participation, and promising to devote what time I might have the following day to the effort. Everyone seemed accepting of my vague reasons for not being active, for which I was grateful.

My guilt somewhat salved, I showered, dressed, and looked at my watch. A half hour to go.

Chapter Twenty-two

The invitees to my little social gathering arrived at staggered times, with the senator still "on his way." Christine and her fiancé, Joe Radisch, and Jack Nebel were already in the house when Seth and I got there. To my surprise, Jardine responded to our knocking. The houseman and I looked at each other for a brief second, not time enough for me to read his eyes. I suppose I couldn't blame him for being angry with me, although his presence indicated he hadn't been detained very long by the police. He disappeared immediately, and Seth and I joined the others in the large room overlooking the terrace. Mrs. Martinez had ignored my comment that luncheon wasn't necessary. A buffet had been set up in a corner, along with a portable, unmanned bar.

Ms. Marshall-Miner, Congressman James Barzelouski, and lobbyist Walter Grusin stood together near the bar. With them, to my surprise, were press secretary Sandy

Teller and Nebel's attorney, Hal Duncan, neither of whom had been invited, at least by me. Carraway was alone by the fireplace, pacing up and down. Christine and her fiancé sat on a love seat near the entrance to the room. I saw through the window that Detective Moody and Jack Nebel were together on the terrace.

"I'll be back in a minute," I told Seth, who nodded and approached the group at the bar.

"Mrs. Fletcher," Moody said as I came through the French doors.

"Hello, Detective," I said. "Hello, Jack."

"Hello, Mrs. Fletcher."

"I think this young man might like to have a word with you," said Moody. "I'll wait down at the dock. Don't want my presence to make the guests jittery. Besides, I always enjoy a few peaceful moments by the water."

When Moody had disappeared down the stairs, I asked Jack, "What did you want to say?"

"About the blow poke, Mrs. Fletcher." He shifted from one foot to the other. "I'm sorry I sounded angry on the phone."

"That's quite all right. What about the blow poke?"

He was obviously uncomfortable, and I didn't press. Finally he said, "When he questioned me—the detective—I denied doing it."

"Doing what?"

"Giving the blow poke to Jardine to get rid of."

"Which wasn't true."

"Not exactly. No. I just told him—Moody—that I wanted to change my story. He said that if I'd lied earlier,

I could be prosecuted for obstruction of justice, and for giving false statements to the police."

"What he says is true," I said.

"I don't want to be prosecuted for anything, Mrs. Fletcher. I might have done something stupid, but I didn't mean to break any laws."

"Be that as it may," I said, "the only sensible thing for you to do is to tell the truth. Why *did* you try to get rid of the murder weapon?"

"Because . . ." He looked through the window into the room, where the others were waiting, before saying, "Because I thought my dad killed her."

My silence confirmed for him that, all things considered, it wasn't a far-fetched assumption.

"But I don't anymore. He swore to me he didn't kill her, and I believe him."

"Did you think that your father murdered Nikki because of the alleged affair between them?"

"Yeah. But there was more."

"Such as?"

"The note."

"Do you mean Nikki's threatening letter to your father?" I asked. How did he know about that?

"What letter? No. There was a note. I found a piece of white paper in Nikki's hand when I discovered her body."

That was news to me. "What did the note say?" I asked.

"It told Nikki to meet him on the dock."

"Was it your father's handwriting?"

"I don't know. It was printed. He signed it 'W', but anyone could pretend to be him, couldn't they?"

"Maybe."

"I panicked. He's my father, a United States senator, and I was afraid he'd murdered his top aide at our own house. I didn't know what to do. The blow poke was lying on the dock. I grabbed it, took Jardine aside, and told him to go out in the boat and dump it in the river."

"What did you do with the note?" I asked.

"Tore it into little pieces and flushed it down the toilet." He didn't allow me to respond. "I know, I know, I know," he said. "I made a big mistake. But can you understand why I did it?"

Understand? Perhaps. Condone? No.

"You've told Detective Moody this?"

He nodded. "Just before you arrived. He told me he knew I was lying when I went to headquarters, and urged me to tell the truth. Will you speak to him about not bringing any kind of charges against me?"

"I don't have any control over that, Jack, but I will urge him to consider the fact that you've now come forward with the truth, even if it puts your father in a bad light. Why don't you get Detective Moody to come back up to the house? I'd like him present."

"Are you going to say that my father killed Nikki?"

"Let's leave that for later," I said. "Go on, now; get the detective."

I reached in my bag for a notebook and tore out a page. When I reentered the room, Senator Nebel had arrived. He strode over to me.

"All right, Jessica," he said. "We're all here, as you wanted. Before you go any further with this parlor game, you should know that I intend to fire Carraway for getting these people here under false pretenses."

I looked to where Carraway leaned against the fireplace. He smiled at me; he seemed uncharacteristically relaxed.

"I'm sorry you feel the need to do that," I said to Nebel.

Barzelouski joined us. "All right," he said, "I showed up because Carraway said we had things to discuss about the power plant. Obviously that's not the case. I understand you set up this get-together, Mrs. Fletcher. I hope you're not going to waste my time. I have important things to do."

Jack and the detective entered the room.

"Then let's get started," I said, "now that everyone is here." I turned and faced the room. "Ladies and gentlemen," I said, "I'd appreciate your attention."

There were mutters of discontent and confusion, but they eventually grew quiet.

"As you know," I said, "I write novels about crime. And on occasion I have helped in a criminal investigation. All of you were present when a crime was committed, when Nikki Farlow was murdered on the dock. I had the misfortune to be the first one to find her body. At least I thought I was the first one." I looked at Jack, who avoided my gaze. "Detective Moody, from the Fairfax County police, has been investigating the murder," I said, "and has been good enough to bring me into his confidence. Because of that, I believe I've learned who the killer is." I looked from face to face. "One of you in this room murdered Nikki Farlow in cold blood."

There was a stunned silence.

"There are plenty of motives to go around," I said, "and that's the place all investigators start, identifying those with a motive to kill."

"This is nonsense," Barzelouski snarled from where he stood with Gail Marshall-Miner and Walt Grusin. "Come on. Get to the point."

I was about to continue when a door to the room opened and Pat Nebel stepped through it.

"Hello, Pat," I said.

"I hope I'm not intruding," she said.

"Oh, no," I said, "not at all. I was hoping you'd join us."

Her husband stepped toward her, but she turned her back on him and joined Christine and her fiancé, Joe Radisch.

I again addressed others in the room. "There are many here who assumed that the senator killed Nikki."

"That's preposterous," said Nebel.

"Not really," I said. "There were the rumors of your affair with her, and she'd written you a threatening letter. She had at her disposal the wherewithal to derail your run for a third term. No, it was logical to look to you as the prime suspect, Senator—or someone doing your bidding."

He flashed a smile and took in the others in the room. "But you all know I treasured Nikki's service to me and to the country. I certainly could never have killed her. Besides—and the press has already written about it— Nikki was a lesbian. An affair between us? Out of the question. Impossible."

"I agree," I said. "But she had other things to threaten you about, didn't she?"

His smile faded to a scowl. "What does *that* mean?"

"That means money," I said.

"Money? What the hell are you talking about?"

"She knew you'd been taking payoffs from special interests, and tried to force you to stop the practice."

For the first time Nebel appeared flustered, at a loss for words. He licked his lips and looked around the room for support. "Lies," he said. "It's all lies. You must be working for my enemies."

"Your affair with Nikki was a lie," I said, "a lie your family believed until a reporter for the *Post* revealed Nikki's sexual orientation." I turned to Mrs. Nebel. "Isn't that right, Pat?"

"If you're suggesting, Jessica, that I killed Nikki because I believed she was having an affair with my husband, you're terribly mistaken. I've adapted quite nicely to my husband's peccadilloes."

"Pat!" Nebel snapped. "That's enough!"

"No, *I've* had enough," Marshall-Miner announced. "I'm leaving."

"Has Mom hit too close to home, Gail?" Christine Nebel said to the congresswoman. She got up from where she'd been sitting with her fiancé and approached Marshall-Miner. "I know all about you and Daddy dearest," she said.

"I don't know what you're talking about," Marshall-Miner said.

For a moment I thought they were about to come to

blows. Sandy Teller stepped between them and said, "Hey, hey, let's calm down. Consider this a game, sort of like charades." He looked at me. "I don't know why you're obsessed with slandering the senator and others in this room, Mrs. Fletcher, but you're way off base."

"Spoken like a true press secretary to a United States senator," I said. "I appreciate your loyalty to your boss and to your job. But you might not be able to spin yourself out of this one, Mr. Teller. Don't misunderstand. What I'm saying doesn't give me any pleasure or satisfaction. I believe in my government and my elected officials. I trust them to do what's right for the country, and that doesn't include taking payoffs to support a lavish lifestyle."

"Now, see here—" Nebel began.

I raised my hand to silence him. "Even so, I would not have pursued accusations of graft and payoffs were they not a pivotal element of Nikki Farlow's murder. I'd make my feelings known in the voting booth back home in Maine."

"Come on," Grusin said to Marshall-Miner. "I'm out of here with you."

"Me, too," said Barzelouski.

"How fitting," I said.

Grusin spun around and confronted me. "What do you mean by that?" he demanded.

"All the guilty parties want to leave together," I said. "You're not going with them, Senator?"

"Don't answer that," said Hal Duncan, Nebel's attorney. Showing some life for the first time, he went to the buffet, picked up half a sandwich, and took a large bite. He swallowed, pronounced it tasty, and said, "I've found this all extremely entertaining, Mrs. Fletcher. It's like one of those interactive dinner theater murder mysteries: great fun, a good story, but a serious waste of anyone's time. I suggest we all have a drink, fill our plates, and enjoy the party."

Grusin, Marshall-Miner, and Congressman Barzelouski walked to the door. I motioned to Detective Moody, who'd seemed content to take in the proceedings without comment. He stepped in front of the trio. "Don't you want to hear the end of the story?" he asked. "I think you'd best stay a little longer."

Barzelouski turned red in the face. "I've had enough of you," he said to Moody. "Get out of my way."

Moody held his ground, but glanced back at me as though seeking a reason for the stand he was taking.

"Mr. Grusin," I said, "of everyone here, I think you have the most reason to stay."

He looked at each person in the room, laughing away what I'd said, hands in motion, head shaking, shoulders hunched, making the point without stating it that I was obviously and overtly demented. When he was finished posturing, he again faced me. "So, Mrs. Fletcher, tell me, what exactly am I accused of? I barely knew the woman. Surely you don't think I killed the senator's aide."

I realized the others were poised for my answer.

"There's an old saying, Mr. Grusin. 'Follow the money.' You were the source of payoffs to Senator Nebel, Congressman Barzelouski, and Congresswoman Marshall-Miner. Nikki Farlow learned about the payoffs and started to pressure everyone, including you."

"Prove it!" he challenged.

"It's not my role to prove governmental corruption. Hopefully a congressional committee will look into what I'm charging and take appropriate action."

He glared at me.

"Why did you lie about your relationship with Nikki?" I asked.

"Relationship? What are you, nuts? Nikki was a dyke."

"Oh? I thought you barely knew the woman. Isn't that what you said?"

He smiled. "It was in the papers, Mrs. Fletcher. You said it yourself."

"I'm not suggesting a romantic relationship, Mr. Grusin. You knew Nikki a lot better than you claimed to me. At the party, when you approached me and my friend Inspector Sutherland at the bar, you ordered two drinks: wine for you, Wild Turkey bourbon with a splash of soda for her. You obviously knew her preference in drinks."

"I may have taken her for drinks once or twice. So what?" Grusin was less brazen now in his stance. "Look," he said, "you didn't know how capable Nikki was of impeding progress."

"Do you mean she was tenacious in wanting honesty in government?" I asked.

"She was about to—"

"You've said enough, Walter," Hal Duncan said. "I suggest that—"

"That no one here say something incriminating?" I said.

"You're treading into an area you know nothing about," the attorney said.

"When it comes to the way Congress works, and how lobbyists use money to influence votes on legislation? You're right, Mr. Duncan. But I do know something about murder."

I returned my attention to Grusin. "You made a big mistake," I said, opening my hand to reveal a piece of white paper folded into a small square. I closed my fist. "You lured Nikki down to the dock with a written note, signed 'W.' "

Grusin paled. "Where did you find—" He stopped. "It's not from me. It must have been Warren. His name starts with a W."

"You must have been in a terrible rush to have left it there."

"That note doesn't prove I killed her."

"Whether she thought it had come from Senator Nebel is conjecture. You share the same first initial. But it was you. And a handwriting expert will confirm it." I prayed Jack Nebel would keep quiet while I bluffed in this high-stakes game.

Grusin looked around the room desperately.

"The question I can't answer," I continued, "is whether you killed Nikki of your own volition, or were asked to kill her by the senator or his Congressional accomplices, who were also recipients of your payoffs. If I had to guess—"

"You don't have to guess, Mrs. Fletcher," Grusin said. "If I'm going down, I'm not going down alone." He turned to where Pat Nebel stood with her son and daughter. "Tell them, Pat. Go on; tell everybody why I did it."

A viselike knot twisted in my stomach.

Pat looked directly at me, her eyes wide with fear, and nodded slowly.

"Did you believe all the rumors about Warren and Nikki?" I asked her softly.

She shook her head. Her eyes never leaving mine, she said, "I had every reason to want her dead. Didn't I?"

I didn't reply.

"I didn't care about Warren's extracurricular sex life. If he wanted to sleep with her, go ahead. But she was about to expose the payoffs. I would be humiliated in the press again. I would lose my home, my standing in the community. My husband would go to jail. She was going to ruin my life and the lives of my children. I wanted her gone. I couldn't do it myself, and asked Walter to do it for me—for us, for this family. Despite Warren's indiscretions, my family means everything to me. So yes, I suggested to Walter that we would all be better off without Nikki." She faced Grusin. "I didn't mean for you to kill her. I thought you might be able to buy her off, use her sexual secret to blackmail her into dropping her plan to expose the payoffs."

Grusin looked disgusted. "Yeah, right."

Pat turned her gaze to me. "Jessica, you must believe me. I was horrified when Nikki turned up dead. It was my worst nightmare. I haven't slept in days. But I know somehow I'm responsible, and I'm willing now to acknowledge my role in it."

She pulled herself to her full height, took in each person in the room, and walked through the door, flanked by her son and daughter.

"Pat, I'll take care of you," Nebel said, starting to follow his wife.

Grusin grabbed his arm. "You wanted her gone, too. Nikki could have brought you down."

Nebel brushed him off. "I never said a word to you about killing Nikki. I'm totally innocent. For too long money has controlled the legislative agenda in Congress. I've done nothing illegal, and the facts will bear that out." He turned to me. "Congratulations, Jessica, on solving another murder. I'm sure this entire sordid episode will provide gist for one of your future novels." He smiled at Moody. "Detective, you've got your man. Now, if you'll excuse me, I have important matters of state with which to deal in the Senate." With that proclamation, he motioned for Teller and Duncan to follow him from the room, which they did.

"I won't take the rap alone," Grusin yelled after them.

"We'll see about that," Moody said. Two uniformed officers quietly summoned by Moody into the house appeared at the detective's side. "Mr. Grusin here is under arrest for the murder of Nikki Farlow." As the officers pulled Grusin's arms behind his back and applied cuffs to his wrists, Moody pulled a card from his pocket and read the lobbyist his constitutional rights. Grusin was led away, and Moody said to me, "Nice job, Mrs. Fletcher. Anytime you want to join the department, give a call."

I laughed. "I may just do that, Detective."

"I'll look forward to it. Keep in touch," he said, and left.

Richard Carraway came to where Seth had joined me.

"You did a brave thing," I said. "I know you'll lose your job because of it. I'm sorry."

"Don't be," the senatorial aide said, smiling. "I'll find another job on the Hill. There are plenty of honest senators and congressmen and -women to work for. I have one favor to ask."

"What's that?"

"An autographed copy of one of your books?" He handed me a card with his home address on it.

"It'll be in the mail as soon as I get home," I said.

Jardine came into the room carrying the day's newspapers, which he carefully arranged on a table.

"Jardine," I said.

He came to me.

"I'm sure what you did won't land you in legal trouble," I said. "But if it does, I'll be happy to stand up for you."

"Thank you, madam," he said. "I am leaving here."

"Where will you go?" Seth asked.

"To family in California. My uncle has a job for me there."

"Well," I said, "I wish you all the best. Thank you for helping me."

"It was my duty, madam." He bowed out of the room.

It was, I knew, the last time I would see him.

"Ready to go, Jessica?" Seth asked.

"Yes, Seth, I'm ready to go."

I stopped at the table where Jardine had placed the

day's papers. A tease at the bottom of the front page caught my eye: RANKING SCOTLAND YARD INSPECTOR VICTIM OF VICIOUS MUGGING.

"Oh, my," I said, "Poor George. I almost forgot. He said he might be released from the hospital this afternoon. Let's go there now."

"Whatever you say, Jessica. Whatever you say."

Chapter Twenty-three

That's quite a shiner you've got there, Inspector," Seth Hazlitt said to George Sutherland.

Seth and I had arrived at the hospital just in time to pick up George, who, despite his embarrassment at my seeing him so bruised, agreed to join us for dinner at a branch of Morton's of Chicago, a wonderful steakhouse that satisfied my two male companions. Seth had joked that a big slab of porterhouse was exactly what George needed for his blackened eye.

"I'd rather eat it than wear it," George had said, laughing. "Is that an approved medical treatment?"

"Sometimes the simplest things work best," Seth said.

George and Seth were in especially good moods, which was to be expected. George had survived his mugging, although his battered face, and the bandage covering stitches where his scalp had been cut ensured the incident wouldn't soon be forgotten. Seth seemed to revel in my successful resolution of the Nikki Farlow murder, and having the corruption in Senator Nebel's office exposed, regaling George with a long tale of what he'd "missed."

"Do you think anything will come of it?" I asked.

"Hard to say," Seth replied. "If the voters back home are made aware of it, seems to me they'll elect us another U.S. senator."

"You said Mrs. Nebel admitted suggesting that Grusin get rid of Ms. Farlow," George said after we'd been served lobster bisque and sliced red and ripe beefsteak tomatoes with raw onion. "Doesn't speak too well of her."

"I feel terrible about it," I said. "She's suffered a lot because of her husband's behavior. But that doesn't excuse what she did. She says she told Grusin to 'take care of Nikki,' not to kill her. I don't know how the courts will handle it, or what will happen to her marriage to Warren."

"Power does corrupt," Seth muttered.

"But only with the corruptible," George said. "Fortunately, the senator doesn't represent the majority of public servants. At least, I hope he doesn't."

Seth chuckled.

"What's funny?" I asked.

"The way people vote these days, wouldn't be surprised if Nebel coasts to a third term, no matter what he's done. Remember Mayor Curley in Boston? Won reelection while sitting in jail."

"Really?" George said.

"Ayuh. Like I said, you never can figure how people vote. Anything new on your terrorist investigation?"

"No. The buggers haven't been identified yet, although

I'm told there are some promising leads. I'll be following up on those the minute I get back."

"When are you leaving?" Seth asked.

"Tomorrow, I'm afraid," George said, looking at me.

"What about you, Jessica?" Seth asked. "I'll be headin' back to Cabot Cove in the morning."

"I have another full day in Washington," I said, "and I intend to devote it entirely to the literacy program. Tomorrow's the final day for that. I've neglected it too much as it is."

It was over our steaks that I brought up Oscar Brophy. "I promised to help him," I said, "but I don't know what I can possibly do for him."

"Oh, meant to tell you that Oscar's back home," Seth said. "He's out on bail."

"How did he come up with the bail?" I asked. "Oscar doesn't have any money."

Seth laughed. "I spoke with Mort Metzger this mornin', " he said. "Seems old Oscar had a bit of cash stashed under his mattress. Plenty of cash. And some folks passed the hat to make up the difference. Once folks hear about Nebel's corruption, they might wish Oscar had bullets in that gun he was carrying."

"Seth!"

"Just jokin'. "

There was plenty of steak left over, but since we were all visitors to Washington, there was no sense in taking doggie bags. Seth asked the waitress if she had a dog. She did, and he suggested she take the leftovers home with her.

"Dessert?" the waitress asked, and reeled off the offerings.

"Not for me," Seth said, wiping his mouth and pushing back his chair.

"Are you leaving?" I asked.

"Ayuh. I figure you two haven't had much of a chance to spend time together, so I'll drag this weary body back to the hotel and get a good night's sleep." He winked at me. "Red Sox game's on TV, too. Don't want to miss that."

George stood and shook Seth's hand. "A pleasure seeing you again, Doctor," he said.

"I might say the same, Inspector. Enjoy the rest of your evening and have a safe trip back home."

"Thank you," George said.

"And if I were you . . ."

"What's that?" George asked.

"I'd stay outa dark alleys."

"I'll heed that advice," George said with a laugh. "And I might add that you should do the same."

"Don't worry about me," Seth said. "If those punks who jumped you had met up with me, there might have been a different outcome—a *very* different outcome. Good evening."

We watched him walk from the restaurant and both started to laugh.

"He's quite a character," George said.

"And a wonderful friend," I said. "Would you like dessert?"

"Being here with you is sweet enough," he said. "Still . . ."

"Yes?"

"I wouldn't mind some rice pudding. You?"

"Let's make it for two," I said, and slid closer to him in the banquette.